The Evolution of GRACE

THE GIRL WITH THE BUTTERFLY TATTOO

VICTORIA M. HOWARD

Trilogy Christian Publishers
A Wholly Owned Subsidiary of Trinity Broadcasting Network
2442 Michelle Drive
Tustin, CA 92780
Copyright © 2024 by Victoria M. Howard
Scripture quotations marked ESV are taken from the ESV® Bible (The Holy Bible, English Standard Version®), copyright © 2001 by Crossway Bibles, a publishing ministry of Good News Publishers. Used by permission. All rights reserved. Unless otherwise indicated, all Scripture quotations are taken from the King James Version of the Bible. Public domain.
All rights reserved, including the right to reproduce this book or portions thereof in any form whatsoever.
For information, address Trilogy Christian Publishing
Rights Department, 2442 Michelle Drive, Tustin, Ca 92780.
Trilogy Christian Publishing/ TBN and colophon are trademarks of Trinity Broadcasting Network.
For information about special discounts for bulk purchases, please contact Trilogy Christian Publishing.
Trilogy Disclaimer: The views and content expressed in this book are those of the author and may not necessarily reflect the views and doctrine of Trilogy Christian Publishing or the Trinity Broadcasting Network.

10 9 8 7 6 5 4 3 2 1

Library of Congress Cataloging-in-Publication Data is available.
ISBN 979-8-89333-109-7
ISBN 979-8-89333-110-3 (ebook)

This is a work of fiction. Names, characters, and events are strictly the products of the author's imagination. Any resemblance to actual persons—living or dead—or actual events is purely coincidental. Author and publisher are not responsible for anything that may be inaccurate.

No part of this book can be copied or reproduced unless approved by the author or publisher.

For my Lord and Savior, Jesus Christ

TABLE OF CONTENTS

Part I: The Dawning of a New Legacy 9
    Chapter 1. 35
    Chapter 2. 47
    Chapter 3. 59
    Chapter 4. 67

Part II: The Girl with the Butterfly Tattoo. 75
    Chapter Five 77
    Chapter Six 85
    Chapter Seven 93
    Chapter Eight 107

Part III: Divine Intervention 117
    Chapter 9. 119
    Chapter 10. 127
    Chapter 11. 137
    Chapter 12. 145
    Chapter 13. 155

Part IV: Sweet Redemption 165
    Chapter 14. 167
    Chapter 15. 173
    Chapter 16. 183
    Chapter 17. 191

Part V: The Butterfly Sanctuary **195**
    Chapter 18. 197
    Chapter 19. 207
    Chapter 20. 217
    Chapter 21. 225
    Chapter 22. 235
    Chapter 23. 243
Part VI: A Destiny Fulfilled **249**
    Chapter 24. 251
    Chapter 25. 257
    Chapter 26. 261
Epilogue **265**
About the Author **271**

PART I:

THE DAWNING OF A NEW LEGACY

JULY 4, 1954

PALERMO, SICILY

It was a hot, balmy day in July when Sophia Grace Gambino entered the world. Lying on a cutting table in the back room of Gambino's Supermercato, Gina Gambino, the only child of the don of Sicily's Cosa Nostra, went into premature labor.

The single mother-to-be had been preparing the family's famous Gambino Sauce when a trickle of warm fluid dribbled down her leg.

At first, the naïve girl ignored it, thinking it was leaky urine she had become accustomed to during her third trimester, but when her water broke, Gina cried, "*Mama, il bambino sta arrivando!*"

The subtle labor pains that started in her lower back quickly intensified. If this were any indication of how the baby's life would be, the good Lord couldn't have painted a more accurate picture.

Unwed and seventeen, Gina Gambino was the hapless victim of a brief but doomed illicit affair. When she went into labor four weeks early, Gina's mother, Anna, summoned the village midwife for assistance. It would have been safer if Gina had been transferred to St. Joseph's Hospital, but her father would not allow it.

Gina's father, Vito, was the godfather of the powerful Gambino family. When Gina became pregnant by J.C. (one of Vito's soldiers), Vito arranged for his daughter's lover to conveniently disappear and shielded Gina like a rabid animal until her child was born.

When anyone asked where Gina was, her father would say she was in Rome attending a private school. His plans were that once the baby was born, he would send it to a New York adoption agency.

As Gina's pains grew closer and stronger, it became more difficult for her to push. After enduring several hours of excruciating pain, the crown of the baby's head finally surfaced. The look on the midwife's face said it all.

"What's wrong, Francesca? Is my daughter okay? Is the baby okay?" Anna cried.

The reason Gina's labor was so difficult was because the baby was in a cephalic posterior position—meaning the head was positioned facing the ceiling instead of facing Gina's abdomen head down. Because of the incorrect position, it made it harder for the baby to get through Gina's tiny pelvis.

"The baby is coming 'sunny-side up,'" the midwife said. "Oh, my God. Look at all the black hair."

Several hours later, the feisty preemie was anxious to escape where she had been living the past eight months.

As the infant dropped, Gina's uterus ruptured, slipping the baby further down into her mother's abdomen and skyrocketing Gina's heart rate.

Sensing imminent danger, Gina called out to God, "Please, Lord, save my baby. Take me home if You must, but let my daughter live. The sin is mine—not hers. She is an innocent victim who was conceived from my stupidity believing a man's lies. I truly loved J.C., but sadly, he did not feel the same."

As the baby emerged, eclampsia set in, sending high levels of protein into Gina's urine, damaging her kidney, and filling her lungs with fluid, causing shortness of breath.

Gasping for air, Gina began to convulse.

"*Santa Madre di Dio!*"

"What's happening? What's wrong with my daughter?" cried Anna.

"Eclampsia! I must take the baby now!" Francesca said.

The midwife acted quickly to remove the baby from her mother's womb. After cutting the umbilical cord, Francesca placed the petite but alert infant onto Gina's swollen bosom. As the newborn raised her wobbly head to gaze into her mother's dark eyes, Gina Gambino breathed her last breath.

INTRODUCTION

In the early 1900s, Palermo was an enchanting town ruled by the Sicilian Cosa Nostra. Noted mostly for its history, culture, architecture, and gastronomy, Palermo was controlled by the Kingdom of Spain from 1479 to 1713 and by Austria from 1720 through 1734.

Located in the northwest part of the island of Sicily, the town of Palermo played an important role throughout its existence. The Cosa Nostra, or Mafia, as it was commonly known, was a criminal organization that had been operating on the island of Sicily since the nineteenth century.

Their core activity was racketeering, drugs, and prostitution. Driven by power, greed, and money, the Gambino family controlled the entire western Sicilian phenomenon.

Vito Gambino, the newly *acknowledged* crime boss, was a tyrannical ruler known as *Crudele*, for his heart was as cold as the Antarctic ice. It was said that Vito would murder his own mother if needed, but thankfully, it never came down to that.

Vito's grandfather Luigi founded and ruled the illegal organization in the late 1800s, but when he became too ill due to bone cancer, Luigi passed all duties to his son Gino.

For two years, Gino successfully reigned until rivals from the Gucci family ambushed and murdered him while he attended Sunday mass.

Next in line was Gino's eighteen-year-old son Vito. Although he was quite young, Vito would one day become known as the most ruthless but successful Mafia boss in the Sicilian mafioso history.

Once acknowledged, Vito chose his team, appointing an underboss (a second in command), a consigliere (an advisor or right-hand man), a *capo dei capi*, also known as captain (a lieutenant), and several *soldatos* (soldiers).

Despite being a ruthless crime organization, most members of the Mafia are brought up Roman Catholic. They may not attend church or live a modest life serving God, but they try to rationalize their behavior to fit into how God should view them.

When one becomes a "made man" (a member of the Mafia), part of the oath is the Mafia family comes first, even before his birth family and God.

The Vatican knew of all the murders that were committed by the crime family. Pope Giuseppe begged them to halt the senseless killings, saying Christians must choose between self-love and selflessness.

"You must choose between God and the organization. Those belonging to the Mafia are not living as Christians because, with the life they chose, they blaspheme the name of God who is love."

The Vatican had been on a crusade to stop these senseless killings ever since one of their own was murdered in cold blood by the crime organization.

In 1937, Father Giuseppe Scalieri was gunned down as he entered his house. At that time, Vito was the presiding godfather, so it was assumed he ordered the hit.

Of course, the incident was swept under the rug, for the organization had *la polizia* in their pocket.

***

When Vito Gambino was twenty-one years old, a village girl named Annalisa Cammora caught his eye. The raven-haired beauty was unlike any other girl he had ever met, for she emanated elegance yet innocence.

The moment Vito locked eyes with the seventeen-year-old, his heart skipped a beat, and his cold, cold heart began to melt (as much as it could). This was unlike Vito, for he could have any girl in Palermo.

To Vito, as with most of the other Sicilian men, women were created to have their babies, cook their dinner, and clean their houses. And the *uomo*'s favorite sport wasn't soccer or rugby—it was courting and seducing women!

Most Sicilian men treat their women badly and insist on society's rights to view them as "sex objects." They believed that wives should be barefoot, pregnant, and turn their cheeks to their infidelity.

So what was it about this young beauty that literally knocked the socks off of Vito Gambino? After seeing the *sultry* beauty, he just *had* to have her, so he sent his mother, Francesca, to meet the girl's family and make them an offer they couldn't refuse. You see, it didn't matter if Anna loved Vito or not, for *made marriages* were not unusual during that era.

Needless to say, Anna's parents were thrilled that the most powerful man in Palermo chose their daughter to be his wife.

Of course, everything in life comes with a price, so in exchange for their daughter's hand, the Cammoras would be protected and financially taken care of for the rest of their lives. Immediately after finalizing the deal, a substantial dowry was bestowed on the Cammoras.

Six months later, the nuptials took place. The ceremony was held at the Immacolata Concezione al Capo, and the reception took place at the Tenuta di Ripolo.

Twelve bridesmaids wore pink gowns and held the traditional sweet pea bouquets, while Anna donned a Claudio Bellini gown and carried an assortment of white and pink roses intermingled with hints of aromatic lavender.

Continuing the Italian tradition, Anna wore no gold or jewelry other than the tiara headdress attached to a thirty-foot Swarovski-jeweled train.

Over five hundred people from "all walks of life" came to see the young couple wed. The A-list included movie stars, fashion designers, diplomats, and a few high-powered politicians.

High security measure was taken as dozens of guards walked the grounds, ready to accost anyone who got out of line or any uninvited visitor should appear.

The guests danced, laughed, and ate the finest food served by handsome, Italian tuxedo-clad waiters. Displayed on Ceramiche La Giara (hand-painted dinnerware) were caponata, swordfish carpaccio, arancini, pasta alla Norma, filet mignon, lobster thermidor, chicken cordon bleu, roasted lamb, lobster ravioli, oysters, shrimp cocktail, and a diversity of canapés.

After dinner, a variety of delectable desserts was offered to those who had a sweet tooth, such as bubble of meringue, chocolate roundabout stuffed with raspberries and cassata, and *la regina della festa*—a grandiose ten-tier wedding cake filled with mascarpone, cocoa lemon, and ricotta.

In 1936, prohibition was in full swing, banning alcohol, but since this was not just *any* wedding (it was considered a *royal* wedding), crates of Dom Perignon and Louis Roederer Cristal were flown in from Christie's of New York.

When dinner was over, the traditional breaking of the cake above the bride's head took place—a practice of wishing good luck to the couple.

The newlyweds ate a few crumbs in a custom known as *confarreatio* (eating together) before the guests gathered the crumbs as a token of good luck.

The reception dragged into the early morning hours.

As the newlyweds stepped into the carriage pulled by four white Lipizzaner stallions en route to a secret honeymoon destination, rainbow confetti was thrown as dozens of white doves in cages were set free to soar the sky.

The carriage was an exquisite hand-painted Ascot Landau designed by one of Italy's top artists. The doors displayed two-dimensional, very brightly colored scenes, and the wheels were an enchanting work of art.

The horses entrusted to drive the newlyweds looked regal in the royal colors of purple and gold as they patiently stood waiting for the arrival of the newly married couple.

Although the new Mr. and Mrs. Gambino made a striking couple, they were as different as night and day. Anna was a believer and devout Christian, and although Vito had been raised Roman Catholic, he defied God, for in his eyes, *he* was God and thought everyone should bow down to him.

In the late 1930s, the Gambinos were the first in Italy to become involved with a new illegal drug called heroin. As soon as he was *appointed* godfather, Vito began exporting the lethal drug to the United States, assigning J.C. Castalano, one of his best soldiers, to oversee the operation.

One day, when J.C. was at the Gambino estate, Vito's sixteen-year-old daughter Gina entered the room. Awed by her innocence, J. C. began to silently court her.

During that era, it was an acceptable Sicilian thing, or an *Italian trend*, for a married man to have another woman (known as a *goomah*) on the side. Forgetting to mention that he was already "married with three children," the besotted girl fell head over heels in love with the deceitful philanderer.

Whenever Castalano was summoned to the Gambino estate for business, he and Gina would sneak off, and within a few months, the teen discovered she was pregnant.

When Gina told her mother, Anna got down on her knees and prayed to God for His protection. Terrified of how her husband would react, the protective mother kept their secret as long as she could, but several months later, when Gina developed a conspicuous baby bump, they could no longer conceal the love child.

Furious, Vito sent his men to find the father-to-be (who had fled Sicily and relocated to Rome), fit him with cement shoes, and feed him to the sharks.

J.C. Castalano conveniently *disappeared,* never to be seen or heard of again. It was not so much that J.C. impregnated his only daughter that infuriated the don—but it was the lack of disrespect and loyalty Castalano had for him and the family.

For the next four months, Gina Gambino was forced to live like a fugitive in the back room of her family's *supermercato,* cut off from everyone and forbidden to have contact with anyone but her parents.

When baby Sophia Grace was born four weeks early, she emerged with a full head of black curly hair and eyes the color of deep emeralds. As the midwife was cleaning the newborn, Anna noticed a small mark on the baby's back shoulder.

"*Mio Dio*! The *bambina* has a *voglia*, just like her mama! I pray this is a sign from God and not a curse from the devil."

"My Gina has been *maledetta* (cursed), and as a result, her life has been cut short. Please, Mother Mary, help this child in the name of your Son, Jesus Christ."

The *voglia*, also known as a Becker nevus birthmark, was shaped like a small butterfly and was located on the newborn's upper back shoulder—exactly where her mother's was.

Vito, the baby's grandfather, also had the exact same *voglia*, as he passed it on to his daughter, who passed it on to her daughter. The don arrogantly called it "the Gambino brand."

Although certain religious fanatics believe a birthmark is a sign of the devil, for Christians, birthmarks have been interpreted as a sign of God's grace and favor. Anna believed her granddaughter was a special gift sent from God destined for greatness.

After Gina held her daughter for the first and only time, the baby was swaddled in a blanket and handed over to Anna, the matriarch of the family.

Seeing the pain in her daughter's eyes, Anna prayed, "Please, Father God, wrap this child in Your arms and protect her. If anyone should be punished, it should be me. The chastisement for marrying such an evil man should not be taken out on my granddaughter, for she is innocent like her mother, and I'm sure she will need direction and protection in her life, and I won't be there. I'll always pray and love her no matter how far away she is, but You are the only one who can protect her.

I wanted to keep the baby as my own, but Vito said he would have her killed if I did. He was ashamed and humiliated that Gina got pregnant, especially to a married man with children. Vito said that he had no grandchild; the baby would have no ties with the Gambino name or be an heir to their billion-dollar fortune."

As the baby was taken from her arms, Anna cried, "*Ciao, Bellisima*. May the Lord watch over you, my *bambina*. *Ti amo*."

TOGO, AFRICA
2004

Contemplating the chapters of my life and the many blessings that God bestowed on me, I realize now that all the fame and wealth I once took pride in is meaningless.

Pride is a heart-attitude sin that overflows into one's imagination and activities. It stems from self-righteousness and consumes the person so that their thoughts are far from God.

Material things that are stolen or lost can be found or bought again, but there is only one thing that can never be found when it's lost—and that is life. And I can assure you that the only one who will never leave your side or abandon you is our Holy Heavenly Father.

As I watch some of God's magnificent creatures roam the African grasslands, I thank my heavenly Father for all He has given me. Granted, it hasn't been all smooth sailing, for I've certainly had my share of heartaches, disappointments, and grief, as almost everyone else has.

I never knew my birth parents, so I guess you could call me an orphan, but when I was five months old, a wonderful couple adopted me and gave me the best life they possibly could.

But let's not talk about me just yet. First, I want to tell you about Africa—the place I chose to settle down and the animals who call Africa home.

Today, a large herd of elephants is gathering in the river to cool off from the intense heat. As they drink water, they spray one another with moist river sand. It is really something to see, and if you ever visit Africa, I promise you will not regret it.

Africa is huge. It's the second largest continent, covering about one-fifth of the total land surface of Earth. It is bounded on the west by the Atlantic Ocean, on the north by the Red Sea and the Indian Ocean, and on the south by the mingling waters of the Atlantic and Indian Oceans.

The population is made up of about thirty ethnic groups, and the groups indigenous to Togo live in the north and southwest.

Most of the country's non-Africans, the majority of whom are French, live in Lome, and the official language is French, although it is not widely spoken outside of business.

Togo is still regarded as the "most corrupt city" in South Africa and the poorest continent on Earth. Every year, more than one million people die—mostly children under the age of five, from malaria.

South Africa is a secular state with a diverse religious population, and Africans are the most religious people in the world. They go through religious indoctrination from the cradle to the grave and are not allowed by family, society, and the state to think, reason, or live outside of the religious box.

Christianity is the dominant religion, with 85 percent professing to be Christian. African religion is by force, not by choice, and the children are brought up to believe the religious teachings.

Let's get back to one of the greatest gifts God created for man—the animals. This particular herd of elephants is comprised of all ages, and what an awesome assortment it is. The matriarch, an enormous female, walks downstream as the elephants slowly follow.

Sadly, the ivory trade is in full motion as poachers kill for a carved trinket, and every year, about twenty thousand elephants are slain for their tusks. It breaks my heart!

This horrific situation began during the Mozambican Civil War when both sides financed their efforts by poaching elephants for ivory, and it has continued through today.

Today, I see kudus, ostriches, zebras, giraffes, hartebeests, and spotted hyenas. These animals live each day in fear of becoming the next meal for African pythons, leopards, lions, Cape buffaloes, and crocodiles.

I've always been a huge animal lover, and it pains me when I see a lion devour a baby antelope, but I have to remind myself this is part of God's plan, and Mother Nature is just doing her thing.

Although I know to hate is a sin, I cannot help but despise this particular Mother!

Many times, I've been asked why a loving God allows killing between animals. I tell them that when sin entered the world through man (Adam and Eve), it was felt throughout God's entire creation, which included the animal kingdom. And if animals were not killed, they would rapidly overpopulate and eventually starve to death—and starvation is a much crueler way of dying, for it is not quick.

In the very beginning of creation, God had already established that both predator and prey together are essential for life on this planet. This was nature's built-in mechanism of checks and balances that keep everything in order. And if you saw how many starving children live here, your heart would break as mine does.

Killing the animals feeds the people, so for this reason, I guess I can accept it. I know that in the new creation, there will be no carnivores, so I am looking forward to one day returning home where it will be total love and bliss.

***

As Grace was admiring a baby zebra wade in the water, a beautiful bright blue butterfly landed on her shoulder. Smiling, she looked up to the sky and asked, "What is it you're trying to tell me now, Lord?"

Ever since Grace was a small child, whenever something was about to happen, a butterfly would appear out of nowhere and land on her shoulder, warning her that something was about to occur.

Some people call this a sign, but Grace called it "a whisper from God," and these whispers saved her many times from the burning fires of hell.

Butterflies had always been one of Grace's favorite things, for they symbolize a deep and powerful representation of life. They are graceful and beautiful, have mystery, symbolism, and meaning, and they are a metaphor representing spiritual rebirth, transformation, change, hope, and life.

The first time a butterfly landed on Grace, she felt a strange connection to it. She thought it ironic that she was born with a butterfly tattoo, and a live butterfly would land on her from time to time, alerting her of an upcoming peril.

The life cycle of a butterfly always fascinated Grace. The series of changes in shape, form, and activities that a butterfly goes through during its lifetime is the life cycle, while the complex biological process involved in the transformation from a caterpillar to an adult butterfly is called metamorphosis.

The *life cycle starts* with the adult female butterfly laying a cluster of small round eggs on plants, which become food for the tiny worm-like caterpillars that hatch between four and six days after they are laid.

Stage Two is the larval stage, when the caterpillar emerges from the egg. The *third stage* is the pupa stage. After a caterpillar attains its full-grown size, it stops eating and enters its chrysalis for the pupal stage.

In *stage four,* the chrysalis opens, and the adult butterfly or imago comes out. The adult butterfly has long antennae, long legs, and compound eyes. When it first emerges, its long, colorful wings are damp, soft, and folded against the body.

The butterfly rests and waits for its wings to dry. Once fit for flight, it takes off in search of nectar-producing flowers. While most butterflies live between one and two weeks, some species spend the winter as hibernating adults and survive for several months.

Butterflies transform from caterpillars, and it is said that whenever a caterpillar lands on a person, he should heed it, for the small creature is most likely trying to tell them of an upcoming dangerous situation, but with Grace, it was not a caterpillar but a butterfly.

A person can learn a lot from a butterfly, such as starting over fresh, starting new, and trying something different. In order to come into form, a butterfly develops through a process called metamorphosis. Just like the butterfly, the human body also undergoes a new sensory experience.

Studying the cycle of a butterfly taught Grace that, in life, people experience pain and change. Many people remain stuck in their past and are unable to move on and overcome a negative experience.

A butterfly is a constant reminder that people can start out in life with humble beginnings and survive and thrive if they don't give up. The transformation from egg to caterpillar to chrysalis is one of God's greatest miracles and one of the wonders of nature.

A butterfly always reminded Grace of an angel—a creature that watches over you and warns you of danger.

***

The first time it happened was when Grace was twelve years old. Uncle Ben was babysitting her, and for five years, he had been sexually molesting her. Since he threatened to hurt her parents if she told them, Grace remained quiet. She prayed to God for guidance to show her what to do when a butterfly flew in her bedroom window and landed on her bed. A warm, peaceful feeling came over her as if God was there in the room with her.

The second time a butterfly appeared, Grace was about to board a private plane from New York to Los Angeles to shoot her first *Sports Illustrated* Swimsuit Cover. When she was about to board, Grace realized she had forgotten her portfolio and hailed a taxi. A butterfly landed on her shoulder and remained there the entire taxi ride.

The third time Grace was visited by a butterfly, she was sitting in a restaurant with her roommate when she received a life-changing phone call telling her that her parents had been killed in a car crash.

She realized that whenever the beautiful insect came to her, a horrific situation was about to or had just taken place.

When she arrived home, there was a message on her

phone from her agent saying the plane she was supposed to be on lost control and crashed into the Hudson River shortly after takeoff. If she had boarded, she would have perished along with all the others. At that time, the idea of a butterfly alerting her to danger did not sink in until it happened a third time.

One day, while I was waiting for a taxi in the city, it started to rain. As I stood there in the rain, a butterfly landed on my shoulder and wouldn't get off. Although it began raining harder, the Lepidoptera remained intact.

A pickup truck skidded on the wet road, lost control, and headed directly toward me. Startled by the butterfly, I jumped and fell backward into the grass just as the truck crashed—exactly where I had stood minutes before—instantly killing a man there.

A coincidence? I'm not one who believes in coincidences, for the Good Book says coincidences are not chance happenings but opportunities from God for us to seek His will and purpose. God may use coincidences to direct our paths, answer prayers, or reveal His power and sovereignty.

My mother always said that everything happens for a reason, and no matter what happens—good or bad—God is in total control, so from that day on, whenever a butterfly would land on me, I would stop and listen.

The world we live in would be better if there was more love, tolerance, patience, and humility, and in a "perfect world," there would be no more hatred or war. But as you know, the world will never be perfect because of the sin committed that fateful day in the garden of Eden.

God created a perfect world in the beginning—innocent and free of death and the curse, the consequences of man's sin (Adam and Eve).

But don't fear, for one day, God will make the world perfect again as it once was. In the new earth, there will be no corruption, no death, no sea, no sun or moon, for Christ will be the light of the new earth. I so look forward to that day.

Let's get back to why I chose Africa as my "final home." It's certainly not where my friends would have thought, for I have lived a real-life fairytale.

There are several reasons I chose Togo to live out my golden years. One is the amazing weather, and the other is that it's a melting pot of cultures, an amalgamation of cultures from all over Africa—the communities range from Nigerian to Indian and everyone in between.

Yes, my heavenly Father has provided me with a blessed life as I've sailed around the world with a famous movie director—mingled with the rich and famous—and once even dined with a king. I've been famous, I've been wealthy, and I've hit rock bottom.

As I said before, fame and fortune are not all that they appear to be, for they cannot bring you long-lasting happiness. Once the initial high wears off, stress, anxiety, and heartache set in.

My entire life, I was "searching for love in the wrong places." All the glitz, glamour, wealth, and fame could not fill the empty void that lingered inside.

I longed to meet just one person who saw the inside of me and not just the outside, for outer beauty fades, but inner beauty is eternal.

I endured years of heartaches and disappointments until I discovered I had been searching for love in all the wrong places, people, and things, for the entire time, Mr. Right was right next to me—protecting, guiding, and loving me. Ironically, He also was a King. His name was Jesus Christ.

My name is Grace Gambino, and this is my story.

CHAPTER 1
December 25, 1954
Bronx, New York

The minute the baby arrived at Saint Mary's Orphanage in New York City from Sicily, she was an instant hit. Not only was she the most beautiful infant ever placed at the orphanage, but there was something extra special about her. The nuns at Saint Mary's Orphanage couldn't put their finger on it, but this infant was different than any other.

Yes, she was beautiful—but the word "beautiful" couldn't come close to describing the way she looked. Her olive skin highlighted her emerald green eyes, and even her tiny toes and fingers were perfect. It was as if God had created a "perfect" baby—this baby was as she had an "aura" that permeated His peace and love.

When the infant arrived at the orphanage, she was exceptionally quiet due to the long nine-hour flight from Italy to New York. She was not flown on a commercial flight but on a private jet accompanied by a nurse.

Dressed in a long white gown and swaddled in a pink blanket, the infant wore a pink ribbon tied around her mass of dark ringlets, and her nametag read Sophia Grace, with no last name.

The Catholic nuns began squabbling over which one would care for the newest addition, for she hardly cried and giggled whenever anyone looked at her.

"This baby is a little angel. Why would anyone give this precious child away?" Sister Rose asked the head mother.

"I'm sure they had a good reason. We are not here to question God, Sister Rose. My only wish is that the right couple adopt and give her the best life possible."

Mother Superior walked over and picked the baby up. "Welcome to the world, my child. It is a secular world seasoned with salt: a world of choices shaped and directed by values. I pray your adoptive parents raise you with the right morals and to know and love Jesus Christ."

Although the sisters did not know the specific details, they assumed the baby was someone very special to have flown on a private jet accompanied by her own nurse.

Now called Baby Grace, the tiny girl grew like a flourishing weed, bringing love and happiness to the sisters from the very first day of her arrival.

One day, a couple from the Bronx came to the orphanage looking to adopt. They were in their early forties and had been trying to conceive for years. After their fourth attempt at artificial insemination, Tony Antonelli suggested to his wife Maria that they adopt, for he was tired of seeing her heart break every time an ICI result came back negative.

The Antonellis were not a wealthy family but a middle-class Catholic Italian family who longed to be parents. They really didn't have a preference for the sex but were hoping to adopt an Italian baby to blend in with their Italian heritage.

When Maria Antonelli arrived at the orphanage, the first baby she went to see was a robust six-month-old boy named Gino, who had been living at the orphanage for three months.

Maria felt bad that the baby had spent the majority of his life in an orphanage. Although the sisters doted on all the babies, showering them with love, Maria knew there was nothing like the bond between a mother and child.

As soon as Maria picked up Gino, he began to scream and wouldn't stop until Sister Rose took him from her.

"I don't think this baby is the one for me," Maria told her husband.

"Maybe you should try again. He might have had a moment," Tony said with a smile. "He really is adorable, honey, and they said his parents were both Italian."

Maria walked back to Gino's crib and tried picking him up a second time, hoping for a better result than the first, but when she did, he screamed again, but this time much louder.

For the next several hours, the couple looked at dozens of babies. There was certainly an assortment to choose from, for there were Asian, Afro-American, and Caucasian boys and girls ranging in age from one month to five years old. Just when it looked like they would be going home childless, Maria passed a crib with the name Baby Grace.

When Maria looked down, she saw the most beautiful infant. As the two locked eyes, the baby smiled! It was at that moment the search was over, and as Maria would tell her daughter when she got older, "You won us over with your smile."

Two weeks after visiting the orphanage, Baby Grace left with the Antonellis to begin her new life. Ironically, it was December 25, the holiest day of the year: the birth of our Lord and Savior.

From the first day they brought Grace home, the Antonellis knew they had made the right decision, for she brought more joy than they ever imagined.

The first time Maria bathed Grace, she noticed a small birthmark on the baby's back in the shape of a small butterfly.

Maria yelled, "Tony, come here! Grace has a birthmark of a butterfly. This must be a sign from God. I know Grace is very special, for she is branded with His love.

A butterfly signifies a profound transformation. They not only are one of God's most beautiful creations, but they are renowned for their graceful flight representing a sense of freedom and independence. And a butterfly tattoo represents a connection to one's spirituality and a belief in the cyclical nature of life and rebirth."

The Antonellis were devout Christians who read the Bible daily and listened to gospel music. When Grace turned ten months old, her little legs lifted her up, and off she went.

Her favorite thing was to dance and sing. She would wiggle to the music and especially loved the song "Jesus Loves Me, This I Know" by Anna Warner.

Jesus loves me! This I know,
For the Bible tells me so,
Little ones to Him belong,
They are weak, but He is strong.

As the music played, Grace danced around the room. When the song ended, she'd clap her tiny hands and say, "Way men" (her way of saying "Amen").

***

The Antonellis attended church every Sunday at Christ Fellowship Church, for they believed that *"the family that prayed together stayed together."*

Every night before bed, Maria would read Grace a story from the children's Bible, and by the time Grace was three years old, she knew the stories of Adam and Eve and Noah's ark. It really was amazing that someone so young could remember and reiterate the stories.

When Grace was four years old, her parents enrolled her in a Christian preschool. During recess, the sisters would find Grace not on the swings like the other children but off to the side, surrounded by several classmates and telling them a Bible story.

Because she was intelligent beyond her years, Grace excelled in school. She was academically way ahead of the other students, so when the school year ended, Grace jumped from kindergarten to the second grade—bypassing the first grade.

At first, Maria was unsure if this was a good thing, but the teacher assured her that Grace would get easily bored if left with the others.

In school, Grace learned about the heavenly Father and His Son, Jesus Christ. She would go home and tell her parents how God had sent His only Son to die for all the sinners in the world.

"Mama, I know God loved His Son, so why did He allow Him to suffer and die on the cross?" Grace asked.

Maria smiled. "Ever since Adam and Eve disobeyed God in the garden of Eden, sin came into the world. If they hadn't sinned by disobeying God, the world and man would be perfect. Jesus died on the cross to be a living sacrifice for our sins because man has been corrupted since the moment Adam and Eve took a bite from the apple."

"Why did they do that, Mama?"

"Because the serpent—who was really the devil—convinced them that if they ate the apple, they would be smarter than God. But they weren't! In fact, because Adam and Eve disobeyed God, they were punished and kicked out of the garden of Eden, "said Maria.

"You and Daddy won't give me away, will you?"

"Of course we won't, Grace. Mommy and Daddy waited a long time for you," Maria said as she kissed Grace's head.

***

Not only was Grace extremely smart, but she was one of the most beautiful little girls in the entire state of New York.

She was slender and much taller than the other girls in class. Her long black hair spiraled down her back, and the color of her eyes grew more radiant as she got older—changing at times from green to a turquoise blue.

When Grace was twelve years old, she got the "woman curse"—her menstrual period. Not knowing what was happening, for Maria never discussed the "birds and the bees" with her daughter, Grace assumed she was dying.

All the way home from school, Grace had her jacket wrapped around her waist and had tissues stuffed in her panties.

"Mama! I think I'm dying," she cried as she opened the door.

THE EVOLUTION OF GRACE

Seeing a trickle of blood run down her daughter's leg, Maria assured her that nothing was wrong—she was just becoming a young woman.

***

The first time it happened, Grace was barely seven years old. Uncle Ben (who was not really her uncle, but her father's best friend) was babysitting Grace while her parents were out.

Tony grew up with Ben Abbatiello, and ever since they were small children, they were the best of friends. They attended school together, played basketball on the school team, and always double-dated. Yes, Ben Abbatiello was as close to family as one could be.

When the two men were in their early twenties, Tony met his future wife, Maria, at a local dance. It was love at first sight.

Ben, on the other hand, was too much of a loner and narcissist to ever marry and settle down with one woman.

Ben Abbatiello was a male chauvinist who thought women were definitely the inferior of the two sexes. He would say, "I would never have a woman tell me what to do. Don't let Maria tell you where you can or cannot go."

Ever since the very first day Grace came to live with the Antonellis, Uncle Ben was assigned as her designated sitter, so when Ben asked Grace to sit on his lap while her parents were out, she didn't think anything of it.

As the years went by, Uncle Ben became more aggressive. He would have Grace sit on his lap while he moved her body back and forth until he climaxed.

The first time it happened, Ben let out a loud moan. Startled, Grace ran away, but Ben followed her to her room and sat next to her on the bed.

"I'm sorry I scared you, honey. Please don't tell your parents what happened tonight, for if you do, I will have to hurt them. I love you like my own daughter and would never ever let anything happen to you," he said as he cleaned himself off.

"I feel so close to you when you're sitting on me. This is my way of showing you how much I love you."

Confused and frightened by the man she knew as her uncle had threatened to harm her parents, the seven-year-old made a point of doing whatever Ben asked.

After that first time, Grace begged her parents not to leave her alone with Ben anymore, but they ignored her, thinking she was going through some silly childhood stage.

Sadly, this horrific behavior continued for the next five years on a weekly basis.

Grace began developing when she was twelve years old. Her mother bought her a bra to support her expanding breasts, but she quickly outgrew it and needed a larger size. By the time she was thirteen years old, Grace was wearing a size 34B.

The sight of her protruding bosom excited Ben as he fondled them while pleasuring himself.

Although Grace was now old enough to know this behavior was wrong, she was too frightened to tell her parents.

She prayed, "God, I know what Uncle Ben is doing is wrong, and I want him to stop! But he said he would hurt my parents if I tell them. Please tell me what to do."

Just then, a butterfly flew in through the open window and landed on her bed. At first, the creature startled her, but it was so gentle and beautiful. As it sat on her bed, flapping its wings, a peaceful feeling came over Grace.

The next time her parents left the house, Grace locked herself in her bedroom. Furious, Ben found the key and opened the door.

Cowering under the covers, Grace begged him, "Please, Uncle Ben, don't do this anymore. This is wrong, and I want you to stop."

Ignoring the girl's pleas, the two-hundred-pound man pounced on top of Grace, pinning her down as he struggled to remove his pants. She screamed and tried to push him off, but he was too big and strong for the sixty-pound teen.

Just when he was about to violate the young virgin, Tony Antonelli stormed into the room. He had forgotten his wallet and returned home when he heard his daughter screaming. The frantic father ran up the stairs, flung the door open, and when he saw Ben lying naked on top of his daughter, he pulled Ben off, knocking him to the floor.

"You no good *sporco bastardo*! How could you do this? You were like a brother to me. This is my daughter!" Tony yelled.

"Grace isn't your daughter. She belongs to someone else who obviously didn't want her. I'm more of family to you than she will ever be," Ben said.

After throwing Ben out of the house, Tony held his daughter tight.

"I'm sorry, honey. I never would have left you with him if I knew he was doing this," he said, tears running down his face.

Early the next morning, Tony reported Ben to the authorities and had his friend arrested. That night, Grace discovered two very important things about life. The first was that the devil could appear in many forms, and the second was that she had been adopted.

Grace was twelve years old.

CHAPTER 2

After Ben Abbatiello was incarcerated, that night was never brought up again. The damage had been done, and now the teen trusted nobody—especially the opposite sex.

After seeing their daughter become more withdrawn, Maria took Grace to a Christian counselor, hoping Grace would talk about what had occurred that night. But the traumatized girl refused to discuss it. She was ashamed and blamed herself for what happened and even felt bad that Ben was locked up behind bars.

Every night, Grace asked God to forgive Ben. She couldn't bring herself to hate him but instead blamed Satan. She was taught early on that Satan could appear in many forms. He first appeared to Adam and Eve in the garden of Eden as a serpent, and when he tempted Jesus in the desert (Matthew 4), Satan took on the form of a man.

The demon challenges your faith in God and is not limited to any physical form. He tempts man where he is the weakest by using the seven deadly sins: pride, greed, wrath, envy, lust, gluttony, and sloth.

The devil is an adversary who prowls around like a roaring lion, seeking an innocent soul to devour. Grace Antonelli was the perfect sacrifice, for she was pure, righteous, a believer, and loved the Lord with all her heart, which infuriated the devil.

Although Satan couldn't break Grace, he was not about to let her go. She was the one person Satan wanted to conquer, and many times in her life, this *wolf in sheep's clothing* would tempt her in various ways and various forms.

It was hard for Grace to believe that, at one time, Satan had been an angel. In fact, he was God's favorite angel who was thrown out of heaven into the flames of hell. The demon is the source of evil and sin and seeks to keep unbelievers in a state of unrepentance.

But the problem was that Grace was one tough nut to crack. Her faith and love for God were stronger than the devil had ever experienced before, and the tempter was not about to let this one go. No sir! Grace Antonelli was Satan's ultimate challenge.

***

When Grace turned thirteen, her parents enrolled her in John The Baptist, an all-girls Catholic high school. She was a year younger than the other classmates, for she skipped a year due to her outstanding grades.

Although the other girls liked socializing with boys, Grace did not. She was leery, thinking they would all be like Uncle Ben.

Ten miles down the road from John the Baptist was an all-boys high school called Catholic High, and on the weekends, some of the boys would hang out at the local ice cream parlor.

The interior of the parlor reminded Grace of the television show *Happy Days.* Behind the counter, the female servers wore a full swing skirt, a cashmere sweater, and penny loafers with bobby socks while serving cherry and vanilla Cokes.

Sitting on swivel stools, the teenagers listened to the jukebox while sipping their sodas. Several would dance to the songs of Hank Williams and Eddie Arnold, while others shot pool or played darts.

When Grace was fifteen years old, she attended her first school dance. She didn't want to go, but her best friend Chloe begged her.

"Gracie, you will never meet a boy if you don't start going out."

"I don't want to meet any boys. I'm happy without one. They're all trouble!"

"Aw, come on. Just this one time, Grace. You have to start living a little. Please go to the dance with me. I refuse to go without you."

Not wanting to upset her best friend, Grace agreed.

The next day, the two girls went shopping for a party dress.

Mr. Antonelli drove them to the city, where they spent the entire day trying on various dresses. Chloe opted for a baby blue sleeveless that showed her curves, while Grace bought a long-sleeve dress with a high neck.

"Gracie, why do you want *that* dress? You have such a great figure—why not show it off?" asked Chloe. "I don't want to hurt your feelings, but that dress makes you look like a—"

Before Chloe could say another word, Grace answered, "Like what? A *brava ragazza*? But Chloe—I *am* a nice girl."

"I mean, you have never even kissed a boy besides the peck on the cheek Harry gave you one time. You don't know what you're missing, girlfriend," Chloe said as she admired herself in the mirror.

***

The night of the dance, Grace's parents drove the girls to the school auditorium. As they got out of the car, Maria said, "Both of you look beautiful. Now go have a good time and make lots of memories."

Grace thanked her mother, but when she looked over at her father, he looked troubled.

"What's wrong, Daddy?" Grace asked.

"Nothing. It's just that you are growing up so fast, honey. Pretty soon, you will come home and tell us you're moving away or you met some nice young man and are getting married."

"Daddy! I'll *never* leave you and Mommy, and as far as getting married, the only man I ever want to love beside you is Jesus."

The Antonellis were concerned about the deep faith their daughter had for God. Although they were devout believers, they thought she should be out doing things with her friends.

"You've got to talk to her, Maria. Grace should be experiencing the things a teenager does. She is missing out on some of her best years."

"I agree, but I'd rather Grace be the way she is than doing drugs, having, sex, and experimenting with things she shouldn't. It is a broken world, honey. It's not the way it was when we were young," Maria said.

***

At the dance, Chloe met a senior from Catholic High named Hudson. Ever since the two teens met, they became inseparable. One day, several months later, Chloe confided to Grace that she had been having sex with Hudson and had missed her period for two months. Frantic, she went to the drugstore and bought one of those pregnancy tests, which came back positive.

"Oh no. What are you going to do?" Grace asked.

"I'm going to tell Hudson tonight. I hope he'll be as happy as I am when I tell him about the baby and will want to marry me."

"Marry you! But you're only sixteen years old, Chloe Martino. What are your parents going to say?"

"I really don't care what they say. I love Hudson, and if they don't like it, I'll run away."

The following day, when Chloe didn't show up at school, Grace called her house. Her mother answered, crying.

"What's wrong, Mrs. Marino? Why are you crying? Why isn't Chloe at school? Is she sick?" Grace asked.

"Grace, I don't know how to tell you, but this morning, when I went to wake Chloe up, I found her dead in bed. She had taken the entire bottle of my pain pills, oxycodone, and died in her sleep. Do you know why she did this? Chloe never took drugs."

Grace surmised that when Chloe told Hudson about the pregnancy, he rebuked her. Afraid and devastated by the consequences she would have to face, she probably thought that the easiest way out was to kill herself and her unborn baby.

The entire school turned out for Chloe's funeral. It was standing room only as hundreds of students came to pay their respects. Everyone was crying and wondered why the pretty girl would have taken her life, for Chloe was one of the more popular girls in school and had a lot to live for. Or so they thought.

The minute Grace saw Hudson, she wanted to ask him what happened, but she already knew. Losing her best friend took something away from Grace that she would never get back. It was just another hard lesson to learn in life.

***

After Chloe died, Grace buried herself in her studies. Although classmates asked her to go to dances, football games, and shopping, she didn't have the desire.

It was now her senior year and time to apply for colleges. With her outstanding grades, every school she applied to accepted her. One morning, Grace's father called her into the den and asked her to sit down. As she walked over to the couch, she wondered what she had done wrong.

Neither of her parents had ever raised their hands to her. There was never a reason to, for Grace was a "model child" who obeyed and respected both parents and wouldn't dream of disrespecting them.

"What college do you want to go to, honey?" Tony asked his daughter.

"I really don't want to move too far away from you and Mama, so I was thinking I'd go to a college close by. I want to study medicine, Daddy. Maybe pediatric medicine, for I want to make a difference in the world: to find cures and save people's lives. Especially the children."

"That's wonderful! But Grace, if you want to study medicine, Stanford School of Medicine is by far the best for a doctoral program," her father answered. "And they gave you a full scholarship. Your mother and I couldn't be more proud of you, honey, and don't worry about us, for we will visit you often and FaceTime every night. We really want you to go to Stanford, Grace."

Wanting so badly to please the people who had rescued her when she was discarded as a baby, she agreed to go to Stanford and began making arrangements for the upcoming fall semester.

***

The senior prom was approaching, and each year, John the Baptist and Catholic High collaborated.

Grace was shocked to discover she had been voted prom queen and Brady Roselli—the star quarterback and most handsome boy at Catholic High—was prom king.

"I really don't want to go to the prom, Mama. Maybe I can say I'm sick or something?"

"Why, honey? Being voted prom queen is such an honor. We will go to the city and buy you the most beautiful dress tomorrow. I'm so proud of you. I always wanted to be prom queen, but I wasn't pretty enough, I guess," Maria said. "So you do it for me."

"*You* not pretty enough? They must have been blind. You were and always will be my queen, honey," Tony said as he kissed his wife.

Seeing the deep love that her adoptive parents had for one another, Grace hoped that one day she would find someone who loved her the way her father loved her mother.

The next day, Brady Roselli was waiting outside of school for Grace. Wearing a pair of tight Levi's, a varsity jacket, a pair of Ray-Ban sunglasses, and a Marlboro Light dangling from his mouth, the presumptuous senior resembled a young James Dean. When Grace saw Brady, she stopped, for he was more handsome than she had remembered.

But his arrogance turned her off when he said, "I heard *you* are the 'lucky one' privileged to go to the prom with me."

With a smirk on his face and his head cocked, Brady took a few puffs from his cigarette and blew it into Grace's face before hopping on his Harley. As he sped away, the other girls ran over to Grace. "You are *sooooo* lucky. I would do anything to be in your shoes, Grace."

***

The next day was Saturday. Maria drove Grace to the city, and the two shopped till they dropped in trendy boutiques on Madison Ave. Every dress Grace would try on, she nixed, saying it was either too short or showed too much cleavage.

"Gracie, you have to buy something fit for a queen. The dresses you pick are too matronly. Your picture is going to be on the front cover of the local newspaper, so please buy something that shows off those beautiful eyes."

Grace finally settled on a turquoise mid-length dress. Although the dress covered her completely, it couldn't hide the curves that the sixteen-year-old had—and there were plenty.

The night of the prom, Brady picked up Grace in a chauffeur-driven limo. As he pinned a white corsage onto her dress, Grace thought she smelled liquor on her date's breath and prayed that her father hadn't.

All the way to the auditorium, Grace didn't utter one word. Brady didn't seem to notice, for he was too busy placing some kind of white powder on a tray, then snorting it into his nose through a rolled up hundred dollar bill.

Grace thought it was baking powder and couldn't understand why anyone would want the leavening agent in his nose.

After finishing inhaling all six lines, Brady turned to Grace and said, "Hey, whatever your name is, do you want to try this? This stuff is the bomb!"

"What is it? Is it baking powder?" Grace innocently asked.

"You *are* kidding me. I mean, I knew you were shy and a

bit of a weirdo, but everyone knows what cocaine is. Come on, try it—you'll like it," he said, wiping his nose. "It's a great aphrodisiac and really increases your sex drive."

Grace was quiet the remainder of the drive and wished she hadn't come. She was still a virgin, and other than a peck on the cheek Harry Wilson gave her one time, she never kissed a boy. Afraid that Brady might become aggressive on the drive back home, Grace concocted a plan to remain in the girls' bathroom all night, hoping her date would find another girl to leave with. After all, there were many girls who would do whatever Brady wanted them to do—but Grace wasn't one of them.

By the time they arrived at school, Brady was high as a kite. Strutting ten feet ahead of his date, the stoned young man immediately began flirting with all of the popular girls, ignoring Grace completely.

Embarrassed yet somewhat relieved, Grace went into the ladies' room and stayed there for the next several hours.

When it was time for the king and queen to be crowned, Principal Miller called Grace and Brady to the stage. As the tiara was being placed on Grace's head, Brady bent down and kissed her, sliding his tongue down her throat.

Some residue from the drug was on his nose—he tasted like an ashtray—and his breath reeked of whiskey. When he kissed Grace, she began to gag, which infuriated Brady.

As the other students watched and laughed, he said, "You witch! You will pay for this."

It was well after midnight when the prom ended, and it was time to go home, so Brady sent one of his female friends to get Grace.

The minute they got into the limo, Brady transformed into a hungry octopus. His hands explored every inch of Grace's body as she tried to fight him off.

During the struggle, Brady ripped the top of her dress, revealing one of her perky breasts. When he saw her large bosom, he became more aroused and succeeded in unfastening his pants.

"See what I have waiting just for you, Gracie girl?" he boasted as she vomited all over him. Luckily, the limo had arrived at the Antonelli house before Brady could react.

When the sedan pulled into the driveway, the porch light went on, and standing outside were her parents. As Grace opened the car door, Brady yelled, "You witch. I *will* get even, believe me," he said, cleaning himself off.

When Grace's parents saw their disheveled daughter, Tony ran towards the car, but it had already sped away.

"Dear God, honey. What did he do to you?" Maria cried.

"Let it go, Mama. I never have to see that boy again."

CHAPTER 3

The summer after graduation, Grace laid low. She never got over the death of Chloe and alienated herself from her other friends. She spent the entire summer at home with her parents and dog, and the only time she left the house was when she went to Saint Joseph's Children's Hospital, where she volunteered on Saturdays.

By the time she was seventeen, Grace Antonelli learned three heartbreaking lessons about life. *First*—you can never trust anyone—especially someone you thought cared about you, thanks to Uncle Ben.

Second—having sex before marriage is totally against what God asks of us—and if you do, horrific repercussions can occur; and *third*—Grace discovered that she had been adopted.

So what *was* her real name, where did she come from, and why did her birth mother give her away? These ruminated thoughts went through her mind like a broken record.

Several times growing up, Grace felt something was not exactly how it appeared. She didn't physically look like either of her parents, and when she would ask them things regarding her birth, Maria would always change the subject.

"Don't you think Grace has the right to know that she was adopted, Maria?" Tony asked his wife one day.

"Why? We don't know who her birth parents are, so if she wants to meet them, we wouldn't know where to start."

"Why do you think it was such a hush-hush secret? I mean—millions of babies get adopted every year for various reasons."

"All we know is Grace was born somewhere in southern Italy, and in order to adopt her, we had to sign a confidentiality form that we would never pursue trying to find out who her parents were. I mean, what's the big secret?"

"Maybe her mother was too young and couldn't afford to keep her—or maybe the father rebuked her, and she had to be put up for adoption," Tony said.

"Or maybe her parents were murderers, convicted felons, or pedophiles? I don't know what happened, but I do know one thing—I thank God every day that we were the lucky ones to have been blessed with this angel," Maria said.

One day, Grace was persistent. "Mother, who *are* my birth parents? Why did they give me up? Didn't they want me?" she asked. "I have a right to know. What if I get sick? Shouldn't I know in case of a medical emergency? I need to know. You and Daddy are my parents, so whatever we discover will never change the fact that you are the only parents in my life."

Maria knew her daughter was right but didn't know how to answer her. Tony walked over to Grace and held her in his arms. As they both cried, he said, "Gracie, honey. We don't know who your birth parents are. We had to sign a confidentiality form when we adopted you from the orphanage.

"I don't know why it was so hush-hush, but it was. We didn't really care why, who, or how—all we knew is that the moment we laid eyes on you, we loved and wanted you to be ours."

Although she wanted to know more about her birth parents, Grace decided to let it go, for she didn't want to hurt the Antonellis, and besides, it was obvious her birth parents never wanted her.

***

Grace began making plans to attend Stanford University in the fall—although her heart was not fully in it.

She would share a room with another girl in the campus dorms. Grace had always been independent, but the thought of not seeing the Antonellis every day saddened her. She couldn't have asked for more loving parents. They were her best friends and had raised her to be a godly woman with good morals.

But she had to admit she *was* excited to start studying medicine and hopefully make a difference in the world, for when it came to children, Grace's heart melted.

That summer, she decided to volunteer at the local children's hospital. Whenever she saw a child battling cancer, her heart would break. Sadly, some children lived at the hospital, for their parents dropped them off and never returned.

Grace asked the doctor, "Why are these children alone? Where are their parents? Why have they been abandoned?"

The doctor said he didn't have the answer, so from that day on, as long as Grace was at Saint Joseph's, she would be every child's "surrogate" aunt.

When Grace went to the hospital, she would bring toys and candy and read stories from the Bible to the children. They all loved her and looked forward to her visits.

She developed a special bond with them, for she had also been abandoned at birth, and the feeling of not being wanted and loved was something she knew well.

There was one particular girl named Holly who Grace was especially fond of. Holly's mother was a heroin addict who had been living under a bridge when she gave birth to her daughter. When Holly was six months old, her mother, stoned out of her mind, fastened the baby in a car seat and left her on the hospital steps in the middle of the night.

The baby was discovered in the early morning hours in a soiled diaper, malnourished, and white foam coming out of her tiny mouth due to a heroin addiction.

When Grace started to volunteer, Holly had already been living at the hospital for several months. The authorities searched for any living relatives but were unsuccessful.

Holly was diagnosed with neonatal abstinence syndrome—a victim of her mother's destructive lifestyle and exposure to heroin while she was in her mother's womb.

As the frail baby went through drug withdrawal, she would become irritable, have seizures, tremble, sweat profusely, and scream for hours at a time.

Dr. Miller, the presiding physician, told Grace, "The heroin Holly was exposed to affected her brain and nervous system. Dependence is characterized by withdrawal systems when one cuts back on heroin use or stops it completely. Holly has now developed gastrointestinal symptoms that are producing diarrhea and vomiting. She is a very, very sick little girl."

Every night, Grace pleaded with God to place His hands on Holly and heal her.

"You are the *only* one who can cure Holly. Please, Jesus, make her better. She has her whole life to live. You healed so many people, like the leper, the crippled, the blind, and the lame. You certainly can heal this precious child of Yours because with You, nothing is impossible."

For the remainder of the summer, Grace made weekly visits to the children's hospital. Two weeks before it was time for Grace to leave for college, she went to the hospital with a bag full of toys for the children. She was sad to leave her little friends—especially Holly—but it was now time to begin a new chapter in her life.

When she entered Holly's room, a nurse changing the sheets was crying and extremely distraught.

"Where's Holly? " Grace asked.

Before she could answer, Dr. Miller walked in.

"I'm so sorry, Grace. I know how attached you were to Holly, but little Holly is not with us anymore. She was called home to heaven last night."

"*What*? I just saw her two days ago, and she seemed fine. I told her I would be back today. What happened?"

"In the middle of the night, Holly became unresponsive, and her breathing became shallow. As we attempted to help, she convulsed and died. She is now with the Lord wearing her angel wings."

Next to Chloe's death, the passing of little Holly was the most painful thing Grace ever experienced.

That night, Grace asked, "Lord, I know I'm not supposed to ask You *why*, but why didn't You heal Holly? I begged You. I know I'm nobody, but I've lived my life to obey, love, and honor You. First, You took away my best friend, and now, little Holly! It just isn't fair!"

Grace cried herself to sleep that night. Although she had always loved, honored, and worshiped God, the *one* and *only* time she asked something from Him, He didn't listen. For the first time in her life, Grace Antonelli was angry with the Lord.

CHAPTER 4

When Grace arrived at Stanford University, she settled into her dorm. Her roommate Simran came from New Delhi, India.

Simran was a petite, dark-haired eighteen-year-old who spoke very little, but that was okay with Grace, for after she lost Chloe, she swore never to get that close to anyone again.

Simran was also an undergraduate student majoring in medicine, hoping to become a neurosurgeon. Although Grace was intelligent, her roommate's grades were off the charts.

Every night, Grace would FaceTime her parents.

"How are you doing there, honey? How's your roommate? Is school hard? Have you met any nice young men yet?" Maria asked her daughter.

Grace laughed, "Mom! That's too many questions at once. I'm doing fine. My roommate's name is Simran, and we get along just great, and *yes*, school is hard. As far as meeting any nice guys—*no*, I am not interested. I told you and Father that my focus is getting the best grades, and being involved with a boy would put a damper on that, so I am not looking for a boyfriend."

Sensing Grace's agitation, Maria said, "I didn't mean to upset you, honey. I'm just being a mom and hope someday my only child will make me a nana."

Grace knew how delighted her parents would be if one day she would make them grandparents, but Grace didn't think she ever wanted children of her own.

She never thought about getting married, having kids and a house with a white picket fence like most of her friends did.

Perhaps she could be a mother to many children, such as a teacher—but one thing Grace knew—if she ever got pregnant, she could *never* give her baby away.

How could any mother give up a tiny living miracle from God who grew inside her for nine months? What was the reason her birth mother chose to give her up? Was it something horrific, or did she just not want her? She prayed that someday she would find the answer.

***

Grace's roommate was studious, quiet, and mild-mannered. Her family lived in Nepal and practiced Hinduism. The fundamental teaching of Hinduism is that a human being's basic nature is not confined to the body or the mind.

Simran believed that God could be manifested in people and worshipped the deity Shiva—the god of destruction.

She constructed an altar in the corner of their room where she could worship Shiva daily. On the altar were a bell, lamp, incense holder, incense sticks, water container, spoon, kumkum powder, and a container to put the offerings. She explained to Grace that each object is symbolic and has its own meaning.

Every morning and evening, Simran would offer prayers there. The act known as *puja* was done by repeating a mantra as she knelt.

Grace also created a small altar on her side of the room to worship her heavenly Father, God. On the altar was a crucifix alongside a Bible and several candles. Each evening before turning out the lights, she prayed to her Lord, for prayer was very important to Grace.

Although the two girls had different religious beliefs and prayed differently, they respected one another. They became close friends, but one thing Grace couldn't understand was why Simran's family never once called or FaceTimed their daughter.

"Simran, how come your family doesn't call you? I'm sure you miss them as much as I miss mine. I talk to my parents every night, and I've never heard you talk to yours once. Why?"

After a few minutes of silence, Simran answered. "Grace, where I come from, there is no dearth of strict parents. Our parents tend to think they are always right and that we should do as they ask, no matter what. They have a hard time adapting their mind to this dynamically changing world. My father is old-fashioned and very strict. Mother loves me dearly but is afraid of displaying that in front of Father."

Grace felt horrible that she had brought the subject up.

"I'm sorry to have pried. That was wrong of me. I'm sure your parents love you very much. We just all have different ways of showing it, I guess."

***

One day, as Gina entered the room, she saw Simran crying. "Honey, what's wrong? Why are you crying?"

"Mother just called and told me Nani died. My grandmother and I were very close, and I feel terrible that I wasn't there for her."

Simran explained that the Hindu religion believed in reincarnation based on karma. In Hinduism, there are three types of karma: that of past lives, that of the present life, and that of the lives not yet lived. The karma will determine in what entity the person will be born in their next life, with the goal of eventually being released from the rebirth cycle to reach moksha.

In the Sanskrit language, *"moksha"* means "freedom," a state of eternal bliss and emptiness—an endless cycle of birth, death, and rebirth into a physical universe.

"I know Nani will return soon, but I miss her. I was closer to her than I was to my own mother. I just wish I could have been there when she died."

"If she's passed on, how can she come back?" asked Grace. "Once you die, only your body dies, and your soul or spirit leaves and goes immediately into the presence of God."

Simran wiped her eyes. "In our religion, we believe when a person dies, one of two things happens: you are either reborn and will experience life again or be liberated from the cycle of rebirth. Nani always said she would come back as a ladybug, so I will be looking out for ladybugs."

From that day on, Grace didn't say another word about Simran's parents or beliefs, for she didn't want to upset her friend more than she already was.

Thinking about what Simran had said, Grace wondered if someone was trying to contact her whenever a butterfly appeared out of nowhere. Could it be her biological mother or father or one of her relatives?

Another thing Grace's mother taught her was never to discuss religion or politics, for everyone had their own beliefs, and it wasn't worth arguing or losing a friend over.

***

The first few months at Stanford flew by. Grace aced her grades, as did her roommate. To celebrate months of hard work the two girls had put in, they decided to go out for dinner before leaving in the morning for Christmas break. They chose a popular cafe called Cucina Venti Restaurant—an upscale establishment best known for its Italian and seafood menu.

As they were seated, a butterfly flew in the front door when it was opened by a patron. The flying creature circumnavigated around the people until it landed on Grace.

The other people in the restaurant were stunned to see the butterfly sit so still on the young woman's head.

"Oh my! Grace, you have a butterfly on your head," Simran said. "That is so cool. It's just sitting there. In our country, butterflies are regarded as symbols of transformation and change. They represent the soul and are believed to carry messages from the spirit world."

At that minute, Grace's cell phone rang. Not recognizing the number, she was apprehensive to answer it, but something inside told her to.

"Hello, this is Grace. Who is this?"

"Is this Grace Antonelli?" a strange man asked.

"Yes, it is. Who is this?" she asked sternly.

"Are you alone, Ms. Antonelli? Is someone there with you?"

A horrible feeling came over Grace, for she knew that the man on the other end was about to tell her something bad.

"Ms. Antonelli, I hate to tell you this, especially over the phone, but there has been a terrible accident. Your parents' car was involved in a head-on collision tonight with a semi, and they both were killed instantly."

There was total silence before everything went black!

Gasping for air, Grace fell to the floor. That three-minute phone call would change her life forever. Grace Antonelli was seventeen years old.

PART II:

THE GIRL WITH THE BUTTERFLY TATTOO

CHAPTER FIVE

Once the shock of her parents' death set in, the numbness, detachment, and disassociation confronted Grace, and she began experiencing the five stages of grief: denial, anger, bargaining, depression, and acceptance.

Grace immediately booked a flight to New York LaGuardia, for she needed to get home and make funeral arrangements.

Since she was an only child and, having no immediate family to help her, everything fell on the grieving seventeen-year-old.

When Grace arrived at the Antonellis house in New York—the only house she ever knew—it didn't feel the same, for without her parents there, the house was no longer a home: it was a cold and empty shell.

After scrimmaging through her father's papers, she discovered his last will in the desk drawer. The Antonellis' wishes were to leave everything to their daughter Grace, but there was one stipulation: in the case they should die together, they wanted to be buried next to one another at Mount Carmel Cemetery.

Grace never knew much about her parents' personal affairs but that they weren't wealthy. Her mother had always been a stay-at-home mom, so she never worked, and her father was an accountant for a small firm. They may not have had a big house or a fancy car, but they had one thing—*love*.

Her dad often said, "Always thank God for everything you have. We may not have as much money or material things as some do, but we are the richest people in the world, for we have each other."

For the next several weeks, Grace kept busy handling her parent's affairs. She discovered that their house had been paid off a long time ago, thanks to Maria's parents, and her father's Subaru was also paid for, so there were no major outstanding loans. But as far as any savings, there was very little.

That night, when she went to bed, Grace had a heart-to-heart talk with the only one left in her life—Jesus Christ.

"Lord... I know I've been a bit of a rebel lately. I'm sorry I was angry, but after Gina and Holly passed away and then after losing the only parents I ever knew, I was so mad. Daddy always told me, 'God doesn't give you more than you can handle,' so please, Jesus, tell your Father no more! I don't think my heart can handle anything else. Please, God, show me what to do."

When Grace woke in the morning, she felt like a new person.

She was no longer frightened and felt like a weight had been taken off her shoulders. The first thing that came to her mind was something her mother always told her—"When you don't know what to do... do nothing." She realized she had received a "whisper from God" while she slept and was now able to think more clearly.

Grace made the decision not to return to college that year, for that was something else Maria said, "In case of any disaster or drastic change in your life, take a year off to figure out what the next step is."

So that's exactly what Grace Antonelli did.

***

For the next few months, Grace did a lot of soul-searching. She was shocked at how her entire life had literally changed overnight. One minute, she was studying medicine at Stanford, and the next, she was back home in New York—alone, without her parents. Thank God her dog Max was with her, for he was the best companion who never left her side.

Her parents bought Max for Grace when she was thirteen years old. Since she was an only child, they thought a dog would be a good companion for their daughter.

Max was now four years old, and just the thought of one day losing him made her crazy, so she tried to put that thought out of her head. She realized that everything in life must die, but the thought of life without her fifteen-pound ball of white fur was too much to bear.

Maria always said that Grace had a fantasy-prone personality and lived in a fantasy world where everything was perfect, for Grace believed in all the good things in life and discarded the bad. She believed in Santa Claus, the fairy princess, the good witch, and one day, a handsome prince riding on a white horse would rescue her and take her away into the sunset, where they would live happily ever after.

Grace believed that every woman was a queen and every little girl was a princess in the making. Sadly, she would discover that this is not the way the real world is.

***

Her parents' funeral was quick and simple. Nobody was there except for Reverend Snow and Grace.

The Antonellis were buried next to each other at Mount Carmel Cemetery under a tree on top of the hill.

After paying their bills, there were only ten thousand dollars left in the bank. Realizing that the money wouldn't last very long, Grace knew she needed to get some type of job until she figured out what she wanted to do with her life.

The following week, Grace went to the local mall and filled out applications at several stores. She never had a job that had paid her, so she had no idea what she was capable of.

When she volunteered at the children's hospital, she didn't get paid—at least not in currency. The satisfaction of seeing the children's faces light up when she came in was worth more than any amount of money in the world.

A week after applying at the stores, Grace received a call informing her she got a job in the cosmetic department at a high-end department store in town.

At first, she was apprehensive, for makeup was something Grace Antonelli knew nothing about. Outside of a little lipstick and mascara, she never wore makeup. She didn't need to, for her complexion was flawless, and she didn't need that goop applied to her beautiful big eyes.

The first day at Hoffmann's Department Store was a complete blur, for learning how to work a modern cash register and what each cosmetic was for was overwhelming.

Grace was an instant hit at her new job, and after working there for only one month, she was named "the leading cosmetic saleswoman" at Lancomer.

Every day, women of all ages flocked to Grace's section, for her personality and natural beauty drew them in—and they wanted to look just like her!

Of course, that was impossible, but Grace worked her "magic," and when she was done, the ladies were ecstatic.

It was a day in late May when a man approached Grace.

He said his name was Tom Williams, and he was a scout for Barbizone Modeling. Assuming she already had, he asked Grace if she had modeled before.

She laughed at the thought. "No, sir. I'm no model. Perhaps you should go see Rina, who works at Chanel. She is one of the most beautiful women here and would make a great model."

When he returned the next day, Tom Williams brought a cameraman along and asked if Grace would allow them to take pictures while she worked. At first, she was leery, but after the man showed her his credentials, she obliged.

Ever since she was a child, Grace had been camera shy, and today was no different. But that was one of the things that attracted Tom Williams to her. Grace was not only gorgeous, but she was also humble and modest.

Unlike the other models Tom had known, Grace didn't realize how beautiful she really was. The other models were cocky and narcissistic, but this one had no idea of the depth of her beauty.

As Grace began applying makeup, the cameraman began shooting. After the cameraman finished shooting six rolls of film, Tom thanked Grace and said he would be in touch.

A few weeks went by, and there was no word, then, one day, Tom Williams appeared holding a thick folder.

"Hello, Grace. I have some very good news for you. When our boss looked at your photos, he flipped, and it was unanimous. *You* were chosen from thousands of girls to be the new face for Lancomer.

This is going to change your life, young lady. Please take these papers home and have your parents and a lawyer look them over. When you are done, call me, and we will get started."

After Mr. Williams left, all the sales girls ran over, congratulating Grace.

The manager, Paula, shrilled, "Do you realize what just happened, Miss Antonelli? This is every girl's dream. Lancomer is number one in cosmetics and fragrance in the world, and being named their 'new face' will open up doors you never dreamed of."

"But my parents are dead, and I don't know a lawyer. I guess I'll have to call Mr. Williams tomorrow and tell him, 'Thanks for the offer, but I can't do it.'"

"Are you out of your mind? We have a lawyer who represents Lancomer, and I'm sure he would help you. His name is Landon Taylor, and I'll have him call you tomorrow."

That night, on the bus ride home, Grace sat in the very back, immersed in a fog. When Max greeted her at the door, she picked him up and kissed him.

"Max, I don't know what to do. This is a dream of a lifetime, but I'm a *nobody* that has *no one* to discuss this with, and I'm not sure what to do," she cried.

But Grace *did* have someone! She had her heavenly Father.

That night, Grace prayed to God for discernment, and when she awoke the next morning, she called Mr. Williams and set up a meeting.

CHAPTER SIX

Grace's head was spinning, for it was happening so fast. She felt like she was reading a Danielle Steele novel, and she was the main character. One day, she was attending one of the most prestigious colleges in the world, and the next, she was sitting in a chauffeur-driven limousine on her way to her very first modeling shoot.

The last time she was in a limo, it hadn't turned out so well.

She often wondered what happened to Brady Roselli—the young man who treated her like she was nothing but a slab of meat as if she was just another notch on his very long belt. Although Grace found the power to forgive Brady, she would never ever forget that night.

Next to her was her loyal companion, Max. One stipulation of accepting Lancomer's proposition was that wherever she went, her dog, Max, could accompany her. After all, he was the one who had been through everything with her—that is, besides the Lord.

Looking in the rearview mirror, the driver asked, "If I may ask, how long have you been modeling, Miss?"

Grace humbly answered, "This is my very first shoot. I'm really not a model. I'm a student at Stanford studying medicine."

"Please forgive me for saying this, but I've driven hundreds of models for Lancomer, and never once was there anyone as strikingly beautiful as you. I mean, it's not the fact that you are drop-dead gorgeous, but there's something extraordinary about you. I can't put my finger on—but believe me, you are very special."

Embarrassed but grateful, Grace thanked the young driver. She noticed the nametag on the front dashboard read "Antone."

"My name is Grace, and I see you are Antone. How long have you been doing this type of work?"

"I began working for Lancomer two years ago, ever since I moved to New York from my home in Puerto Rico. I was so blessed to have gotten this job, for it pays well, I meet all pretty girls like you, and I have enough left after my bills are paid to send my family money."

"It's so sweet to hear someone giving God thanks for their blessings. That is a rare thing today."

"*Rare*? Who else would I give the glory to? God is the one and only one who has had my back all my life. After my father died, my mama was devastated. We were dirt poor, living in a one-room shack. Mom had three children younger than me, so I became the breadwinner at the age of fifteen.

The only thing I knew was how to drive a car, so I got a job working for the local taxi company. Where I come from, the pay is so little we were barely able to keep food on the table.

A friend of mine named Carlos moved to New York the year before and got a job driving a limo, making big money, so I flew here, applied, and now I earn enough money to live comfortably and support my family back home."

"Wow. That's some story. I guess we all have a bestseller," she laughed.

Although Grace was a very private person and didn't open up easily, something about the young driver made her feel very comfortable.

She said, "I was given away when I was born and never knew my birth parents. A wonderful couple adopted me, but a few months ago, I lost them in a car wreck while I was away at Stanford."

"*You* were going to Stanford University? Unreal! Besides being beautiful, you must be really smart," Antone said as he adjusted his rear mirror. "I never knew anyone who went to Stanford. You are not only gorgeous but extremely smart! Now *that's* a rare combination today."

Antone couldn't stop staring at the raven-haired woman in the back of his limo. From that night on, the two people became the best of friends, and for every modeling job

Grace was assigned to, Antone made it a point to drive her.

***

After Grace got through the first job, she took to modeling like someone who had been doing it all of her life.

Her modeling calendar was constantly booked, for everyone wanted to hire "the new face of Lancomer."

The owner of Lancomer was a fifty-year-old Frenchman named Pierre Devereaux. The first time Pierre met Grace was at Lancomer's Christmas party held at his East Hampton mansion.

It had been one year since her parents' death, and she relocated to New York to begin modeling.

Every Christmas, Pierre hosted a holiday party at his huge estate. All of the top photographers and CEOs were there, along with hundreds of models.

When Grace received her invitation, she rushed to Gucci and purchased a long white dress, black pearl earrings, and a black pearl choker.

As she stepped into the limo, Antone gasped. "Dulce Jesus. Mother Mary! You look like a Greek goddess, Grace," he said.

Shyly, Grace hid her eyes behind her hands as her cheeks turned a crimson red.

"You will be the belle of the ball, but why don't you

leave Max with me while you're at the party? I will take good care of him. I want you to go and not have to worry about anything."

"I really wanted to bring him, but I think I will leave him with you because he hasn't been feeling the best."

As Grace walked inside her boss's home, it was time for her to be speechless, for never in her life had she seen such a magnificent home.

No, this was not a home—it was a palatial estate surrounded by a huge electric security gate, an Olympic-sized pool, tennis court, and guesthouses.

Mr. Devereaux had been waiting by the door for Grace to arrive, and the minute he saw her, he ran over and greeted her by kissing both of her cheeks.

"*Tu es belle. Soyez la bienvenue chez moi*! I have been anxiously waiting to meet you, my dear."

Every Lancomer model was there shooting imaginary daggers at the beautiful newcomer. Although one girl was prettier than the other, Grace was in a league of her own.

As the guests mingled, they munched on hors d'oeuvres and sipped champagne. Grace was not a drinker, and outside of a glass of wine she once had with her father, alcohol always tasted gross to her. She noticed that everyone was holding a flute of champagne, and not wanting to be different, she accepted a glass. To her surprise, she loved the way it tasted and took another. After drinking several glasses, she became a bit tipsy.

Occasionally, Mr. Devereaux would break away from the others to talk to Grace. As the party started to fizzle down, Pierre said, "I want to personally thank you for making my company number one in the universe. Your face has been seen in all corners of the world, and everyone has fallen in love with you—including me."

"It should be me thanking you, Mr. Devereaux, for giving me this opportunity. I will be forever grateful to you," Grace said.

"Then you will start off by calling me Pierre," he said, walking her to the limo.

Anxiously waiting for her in the back seat was her loyal companion, Max, with his tail wagging. Grace picked him up and kissed him.

"Well, how did it go, Grace? I think I know the answer, for Mr. Devereaux has *never* walked a woman to the car before. He must really like you," Antone said.

***

That night, when Grace got into bed, she gave Max an extra long hug.

"Dear Lord, I am so thankful for all You have given me. Thank You for Your love, grace, and mercy, which guide me through every day, and thank You for Your presence in my life, which brings me hope and joy every day. I am so blessed to have You in my life, and I am eternally grateful for all You do. Please watch over my mother and father in heaven, my birth parents I never knew, and my new friend Antone. And lastly, watch over Max and when it is time for him to cross the rainbow bridge in the sky, please make it quick so he doesn't suffer. Amen."

CHAPTER SEVEN

Ever since the night of the Christmas party, Mr. Devereaux made it a point to conveniently show up at all of Grace's modeling jobs. Although she didn't notice his special attention, all the other models certainly did.

Before Grace signed on to Lancomer, their top model was a girl named Tianna—a nineteen-year-old from Negril, Jamaica. The Jamaican beauty towered six feet tall, and her flawless skin was the color of caramel chocolate. Although Pierre and the statuesque model had been having an affair for two years, they tried to keep it under wraps, but everyone in the modeling world knew what was going on.

The exotic beauty was in love with her boss, but to Pierre Devereaux, Tianna was merely a "friend with benefits."

Up until the day that C'est La Vie Jeans hired Grace and Tianna, the jeans company known for discovering Ellie, Grace always modeled solo.

When Tianna found out she was one of two models chosen for the C'est La Vie Jeans ad, she was ecstatic for she always wanted to do one of their campaigns.

She knew that this could be the big one that could make her the most famous model in the world—but there was one thing standing in her way: Grace Antonelli.

The two models were flown by Pierre's personal jet to a private island in the Caribbean, which just happened to be owned by Pierre.

Of course, their boss would be accompanying them on the journey. During the flight, he showered both women with Dom Perignon and the finest hors d'oeuvres.

After the first glass, Grace stopped drinking, for she didn't want the alcohol to affect her senses and performance, but that didn't stop Tianna from gulping several glasses down.

When they arrived on location, the crew was set up and ready to go. Grace was handed a black strapless swimsuit with geometric cutouts, while Tianna got a white sequined bikini.

At first, Grace was hesitant to wear a strapless for it would reveal her birthmark. Up until that day, she had managed to hide her *special mark*, as her mother called it.

Grace wasn't sure exactly when she started to be ashamed of the butterfly tattoo. As a child, she would take a shower for an hour trying to scrub it off and even bought something at the drugstore to fade birthmarks, but nothing worked.

Her mother said the birthmark was definitely from God because she was very special and she shouldn't try to hide it, but as Grace grew, so did the mark, forming a tiny butterfly.

One time, a photographer noticed it and wanted to take a picture of it, but Grace refused.

I was not ready to show the world something I didn't even know the meaning of. I get a feeling—maybe it's one of my whispers from God—but I feel the birthmark has something to do with finding who my birth parents are. I don't know who, when, or where—but until God is ready to reveal it to me, I must learn to have patience and wait.

As Grace and Tianna were changing into their swimsuits, Tianna saw Grace's unusual birthmark and commented, "Better have the makeup girl try to hide whatever that ugly thing is on your back, or else you're gonna ruin our entire shoot. And I don't know about you, but I wanna get this over with as quickly as I can."

Grace got the feeling that Tianna didn't like her. She didn't know why, but she wasn't about to let it ruin the shoot.

The photographer Pierre hired was Marc Chauvier, one of the world's best who had taken photos of every top model on the planet, and to have him photograph them was an honor.

Marc started by having both models stand next to one another, posing them in various ways. First, he had Grace lie on her side while Tianna stood behind her, gazing at the ocean.

When Marc saw the birthmark on Grace's back, he was blown away.

"Oh, *mon dieu*! Pull your hair up, Grace, and look over that shoulder. Yes! That's it," he screamed.

Pierre shot a total of ten dozen rolls of film as the girls changed poses. When Tianna was asked to put her hand around Grace's waist, she blurted, "Why do I have to always be the one who is doting on her? Can't you make her look up to me once in a while?"

Appalled at her outburst, Mr. Devereaux spoke up, "Listen, Tianna, you will do exactly as Marc asks. If you don't, I certainly can bring in another model who would love to do your job."

From that moment, the tension was so thick you could cut it with a knife. After four hours and hundreds of shots, Marc called it a day.

"*Finite! Fantastique!* You two were perfect—especially Grace. You have the face of an angel and the body of a Greek goddess."

"Thank you. It was fun. Tianna, you were wonderful to work with," Grace said as she changed her clothes. Grace was always considerate of other people's feelings and didn't want Tianna to feel underrated.

Once onboard the jet, Mr. Devereaux began doting on

Grace, complimenting her over and over. "This is going to be sensational. I'm so proud of both of you," he said as he offered Grace more champagne. "Drink up, honey. You certainly deserve it."

That was the last straw! Tianna had enough, and drinking half a bottle of champagne didn't help what would happen next.

The six-foot model stood up and threw the remaining bottle of bubbly on Grace's face.

"I've had enough of you, Missy. You think you're all that. Well, when our boss is done having his fun with you, he will toss you aside for a younger model."

Tianna turned to Pierre, "And I wonder what your wife will say when I tell her what we have been doing for the past two years."

"You witch. You no longer work for Lancomer. You're fired!"

Grace begged Pierre, "Please don't fire Tianna. She didn't mean what she did or said. We have been out in the hot sun all day, and drinking champagne certainly didn't help. Please don't let Tianna go."

At that moment, Grace could have asked Pierre to buy her the Statue of Liberty, and he would have, for when Pierre Devereaux looked into Grace's violet eyes, he melted.

"Alright then. Tianna, you can stay on at Lancomer, but one more outburst like that, and I promise you will be finished in the modeling world," Pierre said.

After the plane landed and they disembarked, Tianna pulled Grace to the side.

"I'm *really* sorry, Grace. What you did for me back there is something I will never forget. Nobody has ever stood up for me before. Why would you stick up for me after what I did to you? You saved my job. When Mr. Devereaux fires someone, it's final. He must really like you. I should be jealous because he's now interested in you—but I know he will never leave his wife. I wasted a year and a half thinking that he would. He promised me, and I believed him," Tianna cried. "Be careful, for Pierre will pull you into his web, and when he's done with you, he will spit you out. He did it to me and to Katya Ollsen before me."

"Thanks, Tianna, for caring, but I'm not interested in Mr. Devereaux that way. And I would *never* go with a married man because that's adultery. I'm not judging you, Tianna, but you are so beautiful. Don't waste your life on a married man. There's someone out there who deserves you."

From that day on, Tianna and Grace became best friends, and when someone needed to hire two models, they requested "those two gorgeous Lancomer girls: the chocolate Amazon and the girl with the butterfly tattoo."

And that is how Grace became known around the world as "the girl with the butterfly tattoo."

VICTORIA M. HOWARD

PALERMO, SICILY
1971

When Anna Gambino saw the *Sports Illustrated* issue on the newsstand, she almost fainted. On the cover was the most beautiful woman she had ever seen. At first glance, she thought it was just another lucky model that made the cover of one of the world's most prestigious magazines, but when Anna read the heading, "*Sports Illustrated* Model of the Year. Grace Antonelli—The girl with the butterfly tattoo," the older woman gasped. "This can't be—can it?"

After looking at the photo more closely, the model on the cover resembled Anna's deceased daughter, Gina, but when Anna saw the tattoo on the model's back shoulder, she knew that undoubtedly this was her long-lost granddaughter, Sophia Grace. It had been over seventeen years since the matriarch of the Gambino family held her granddaughter for the first and last time before the infant was flown to the United States to be put up for adoption. Anna never got over losing her only child, and there wasn't a day that went by she didn't think about or worry about her granddaughter, Sophia Grace.

The grieving grandmother called the orphanage several times to find out who had adopted her granddaughter, but she was always told they couldn't divulge that information.

Unbeknownst to her, Anna's husband, Vito, quietly

donated one million dollars to the orphanage in exchange that under no circumstances were they ever to divulge the names of the family that adopted the baby—even to his wife, Anna.

After Gina died and Grace was taken away, Anna had nothing but contempt for her husband, Vito. She knew he was behind the death of J.C.—the man who impregnated Gina and the father of her granddaughter—and it was because of Vito that Sophia Grace was sent away. She hated him with every ounce she had in her frail, aging body.

Anna tried leaving Vito several times, but the tyrant would find her, bring her back home, and once again make her a prisoner.

A woman who marries someone in the Mafia signs a death certificate when she says, "I do." They usually live in a loveless marriage, and their main job is to honor and obey their husband, have children, and turn the other cheek to his infidelities and business dealings.

Some people think that "Mafia wives" have it made, for they are provided for, live a modest but comfortable life, and are honored to be married to someone who is so rich and powerful. But it's not what it seems. Anna learned early on that a mob wife must ignore her husband's extramarital affairs and his *goomah* (mistress), for this is a fact of mob life.

In order to keep the cars, house, furs, and jewelry, a mob wife has to accept the *goomah* and learn to turn the other cheek.

Throughout their marriage, Vito Gambino had many mistresses. The first time Anna discovered her husband's infidelity, she was heartbroken. She called her mother crying.

"Mama, Vito has another woman. What do I do?"

"You do nothing. Let him be with whomever he wishes. Vito takes very good care of you—and also of your father and me!" her mother said.

Crushed that her mother told her to ignore the whole situation, Anna never discussed it with her again. Ever since their daughter married the godfather of the Gambino family, the Cammoras had no more money problems, and for that reason, Anna was grateful and learned to ignore her husband's affairs, but the marriage was nothing like Anna Gambino dreamed it would be.

The day that Anna gave birth to her daughter, Gina, she was totally devoted to her. Being the daughter of one of the most powerful men in the country had some very nice perks, such as driving the nicest cars, being dressed in designer outfits, and never having to worry about getting bullied or abused. Not to mention having your own personal bodyguard.

With Vito in charge, the Gambino empire grew into one of the wealthiest families in Italy, controlling all prostitution, drugs, and corrupt dealings. Although she had never been wealthier, Anna would gladly give it all up to have her daughter and granddaughter back.

Afraid of what her husband would do if he caught wind that his granddaughter was alive, well, and now the world's newest supermodel, Anna purchased every copy of the magazine she could and destroyed them.

Seeing her granddaughter again stirred up Anna's emotions and feelings, so she secretly hired a detective to find where Grace lived and any personal information he could find.

From the day that Anna saw the *Sports Illustrated* issue, she began wiring twenty thousand dollars a month directly into Grace's bank account in New York. The sender would remain anonymous so that Grace could never discover who it was.

During her marriage, Anna received over five million dollars worth of jewelry. Every time Anna caught Vito being unfaithful, he would buy her an expensive piece of jewelry. Although the jewels were beautiful, Anna had no need for them, so she secretly met with a dealer who bought the jewels for cash.

The Gambino empire was worth at least five hundred million dollars, and they couldn't spend it all if they had lived another one hundred years. Having no children, Vito told Anna that if she passed before he did, he would leave every penny to various charities.

"But Vito, we have a granddaughter who is the legal heir. It should be left to her."

"I have *no* grandchild, and neither do you. When her mother got pregnant by that low-life scum, she disinherited any rights she had, and so did her bastard daughter. Don't ever bring this child up again!"

When Anna took vows to "honor, love, and obey her husband," she knew that no matter what, they must remain together as husband and wife until death do them part. Because she was a Christian, she knew that in God's eyes, she must remain married to Vito until the end—no matter how unhappy or abusive their marriage was. But that didn't stop Anna from despising Vito and praying every night he would die.

***

When Grace received the first wire of twenty thousand dollars into her bank account, she thought it must be a mistake and immediately contacted the bank. They told her they had no information to give her other than the wire came from somewhere in Sicily.

Since Grace had no idea who the sender was, she never touched the money. She didn't feel the money was hers and invested it in an annuity her financial advisor had set up for her.

Earning well over one million dollars a year modeling, Grace had no need for the peripety and thought that someday she would donate this found money to a worthy cause—perhaps to unwanted orphans who had been discarded like she once was.

***

It had now been five years since Grace launched her modeling career and had made quite a name in the fashion world. Although she appeared on the front covers of *Vogue*, *Sports Illustrated*, *Harper's Bazaar*, *Elle*, and *L'Officiel*, deep inside was an empty void.

She had everything a girl could dream of. A penthouse in New York Trump Tower, fancy designer threads, and fame and money—but there still was an emptiness that could not be filled.

Mingling with A-listers—famous, wealthy, renowned people, and the many handsome, rich and powerful men she met—not one ever gave her that special feeling she longed for.

One time, there was a man named Blake Corona—the owner of a yacht company who dealt with only the rich and famous.

Grace liked him and had come close to letting her heart go, but after dating him for several months, she discovered Blake had been seeing Mia, another top model, too.

When Grace confronted Blake, he told her, "I've been with you for several months now, and you never gave me what I needed. I'm a man with needs, and being around you every day only drives me crazier. Mia gives me what I need, but she's not you, babe. She can't touch your little toe."

Although Grace was sad, for she did care about Blake, she thanked God for saving her once again from future heartbreak. As her mother said, "Once a cheater—always a cheater," so Grace knew that eventually Blake would wander again.

"Lord, why can't I find someone who loves me for who I am, not for what I am or what I look like? I have so much love inside, but all men seem to want me for is sex or to be a trophy."

CHAPTER EIGHT

Grace and Tianna were booked to do an important modeling shoot for Guess Jeans, and Antone would be the designated chauffeur.

"I can't wait for you to meet my best friend, Tianna," Grace told Antone. "It's about time you two met. I know you will be the best of friends."

"What you talking about, girl? *I'm* your best friend," Antone laughed.

"Yes, you are my best male friend, but Tianna is my best female friend."

When Tianna walked out of the front door of the Waldorf Astoria Towers, the bellman's mouth was ajar.

"G-g-g-g-good day, Ms. Tianna. Don't you look especially lovely today?"

Tianna was wearing a one-piece leopard hooded jumpsuit, thigh-high leather boots, and her long black hair pulled back in a tight bun. As she walked to the limo, she literally stopped all traffic on Park Avenue.

"*Madre di Dio*," Anton said.

When Tianna stepped into the limo, Grace saw Antone's eyes bulging out of his head through the rearview mirror. The young man stuttered, "Hello, M-M-M-Miss. My name is Antone. If there is anything you need—please ask."

As Grace was introducing her two friends, she conceptualized a bolt of lightning, for the chemistry between the two people was electrifying. So four months later, when Tianna told Grace she was going to have Antone's baby, Grace was blown away.

"What? How did that happen?" Grace asked.

"Well, you know how it happened, Grace," Tianna laughed. "The birds and the bees met, fell in love, and a little *bambino* is on the way."

"But what about your modeling career? It is hotter than it has ever been. You are one of Lancomer's top models."

"Gracie, I've never been happier. I love Antone so much, and I know he's the one. I've always wanted a child, and I'm almost twenty-four years old, and my biological clock is running out. And you know that we are both reaching the age when modeling is coming to an end as Pierre is now hiring sixteen- and seventeen-year-olds."

The two women held each other as they cried tears of joy.

"I am so happy for you guys. I love you both so much,

and I think you guys make a beautiful couple and will make a gorgeous baby," Anna said.

"And I have another surprise. Antone and I discussed it, and we agree that you are going to be our baby's godmother."

***

The day after the Guess shoot, Tianna went into Lancomer and gave her resignation. To her surprise, Pierre wasn't a bit upset. After the outburst when Tianna had threatened to tell Pierre's wife of their affair, he never saw the model again.

Although modeling wasn't much fun without her sidekick Tianna, Grace was happy for her friend and looked forward to the birth of her baby.

Getting married and having children was never a priority to Grace. Although she adored children, she wanted to help and be a mom to many kids, not one or two. But how to accomplish that was unknown to her at that time.

With Tianna's departure from the modeling world, Grace began getting more jobs than she could handle.

Pierre began wooing Lancomer's newest model, Kiki, a Columbian beauty thirty-five years younger. Although Grace didn't approve, she turned her head the other way. After all, who was she to judge? Only God had that right. And Grace learned long ago, "You sow what you reap," so eventually, Pierre would have to answer to his Maker—and to his wife.

When Grace met Pierre's wife, Angelina, she felt sorry for her. Mrs. Devereaux was a beautiful forty-something redhead who, in her younger years, had been a top model at Barbizone Modeling.

One day, while attending a party at the Devereaux's, Angelina told Grace, "Enjoy the ride while you can, dear. This is a cutthroat business. They'll love you one day and hate you the next. And when you hit twenty-five, the camera will fall out of love with you, and so will my husband."

Pierre was entertaining in the main room alongside his new flame Kiki. His wife turned her cheek as if not to notice, but Grace could see the hurt and pain in her eyes.

That night, when Grace said her prayers, she asked God to protect Tianna, Antone, and their unborn baby.

"Please, Lord, if there is someone You want in my life, You will send him. If not, I will be content to live out my life the way You want me to. You have given me an amazing life, and I'm sorry if I haven't spent more one-on-one time with You lately, but I know You understand. The only thing I ask of You, if I may, is to one day find my birth parents before I die. In Jesus' name, I pray. Amen."

***

It was at the annual "Model of the Year Worldwide" ceremony when Grace Antonelli's life would take yet another pivotal turn.

The award ceremony was held at the Waldorf Astoria Hotel in Rome, Italy. This was the third consecutive year Grace Antonelli had been named "Model of the Year Worldwide."

Every year, over 250 voters representing a wide range of the industry's top stylists, designers, photographers, editors, hair and makeup artists, casting directors, and bigwigs from Elite, Ford, Storm, LA Models, Nous, and DT Models voted for who they thought impacted the fashion world the most—the singular face that defined the year as a whole with ubiquitous industry demand and presence.

Also, one model would be named Breakout Star. The winner would be scored on who had a substantial presence on the modeling scene that year.

The banquet room was packed solid as hundreds of onlookers stood in the back to watch the ceremony. Beaming in the front row was a very pregnant Tianna, accompanied by her fiancée, Antone. They had flown to Rome to watch their favorite girl once again take home the title.

Due to the fact that Tianna was eight months pregnant, Grace begged her not to make that long flight from LaGuardia to Leonardo da Vinci Airport. It would have been better if Tianna could have flown with Grace on Pierre's private jet, but when Grace asked if her pregnant friend could fly with them, he said there was no room.

She knew it was an excuse, for there was nobody on the plane but the pilot, the stewardess, Pierre, Kiki and Grace.

And the jet easily had room for ten people.

"How are you feeling, honey?" Grace asked Tianna.

"A bit tired from the long flight, but other than that—fantastic!"

"Don't worry your pretty face about our girl, Grace. I am taking good care of her and our little girl, Gabriella," Antone said as he put his hand on Tianna's bulging stomach.

"Grace, hurry over here! Put your hand right here. Gabby is talking to you, honey," Tianna said, laughing.

"I love the name 'Gabriella.' How did you choose that name?" Grace asked.

"The name means 'God is my strength.' And you and I know that He is exactly that!"

Ever since Tianna began hanging out with her, Grace had noticed a huge change come over her friend. Tianna was never a religious girl, but in the past year, she grew closer to her Savior. And the fact that Antone was a believer didn't hurt.

As Grace lightly rubbed Tianna's belly, the baby kicked.

"Wow! She must either be hungry or mad."

"No, she's saying how proud she is of her Aunt Grace," laughed Tianna.

***

The first award was for Breakout Star, and to nobody's

surprise, Kiki Alvarez took home the honors.

As Kiki walked on stage to receive the trophy, Pierre beamed like a Cheshire cat.

Grace was happy to see that his wife, Mrs. Devereaux, was absent, for there was no need to keep rubbing salt in an open wound. It was now time to name the Model of the Year Worldwide. When the emcee announced, "And for the third year in a row, the title of Model of the Year goes to 'the girl with the butterfly tattoo—Grace Antonelli,'" the entire audience went wild.

As Grace walked onto the stage, she saw Tianna fall to the floor. Immediately, Grace jumped off the stage, high heels and all, and ran to her friend's aid.

"What's wrong, Ti?" Grace asked her friend.

"I think Gabby wants to meet us *now*," said Tianna.

"But you are only thirty-four weeks, honey. It's too early," Antone said. "It's not time, little girl."

As the paramedics rolled Tianna out on a stretcher, a man made his way over to Grace.

"*Congratulazioni, Ms. Antonelli. Ciao, mi chiamo Mattia Russo. Sono produttore cinematografico.*"

Although Grace did not speak much Italian, she knew that the man was congratulating her, and for the first time in twenty-one years living on the planet, Grace Antonelli experienced something she never had before—love at first sight, or maybe it was lust at first sight?

"I'm sorry, but I don't speak Italian," Grace shyly answered.

Laughing, the man apologized. "Please forgive me. I forget that most people from America don't speak my language. Let's try this again."

"Congratulations, Ms. Antonelli. Hello, my name is Mattia Russo. I am a film director, and I would like to talk to you about possibly starring in my new movie, *Donna di Dio*," he said in a strong Italian accent.

"The movie will be filmed in Hollywood, and it will begin shooting in two months. *Donna di Dio* means 'a woman of God,' and I think *you* would be the perfect woman for the role."

Grace stood there in shock. Not only was she worried sick about her best friend, Tianna, but the most handsome man in the world had just asked her to star in his movie.

After composing herself, Grace said, "But I'm not an actress. I wouldn't know the first thing about it. Perhaps you should find someone who is an established actress."

"Ms. Antonelli, every day you model, you are acting. And in all my years, I have never seen anyone whom the camera loves as much as it loves you. Here is my card. Please call my office tomorrow and have my secretary Sandy set a time to have you come in for a screen test."

As the Italian director walked out the door, Grace watched his every step. Never in her life had she felt butterflies in her stomach before. Yes, the flying creatures had landed on her many times to warn her of something, but this was different.

While walking to the back door, Grace passed a middle-aged woman crying. She stopped in front of the woman and smiled. Although Grace was certain she didn't know her, there was something about the woman that looked oddly familiar. Grace couldn't put her finger on it, but this woman oddly touched her.

The elderly woman returned the smile and gently touched Grace's hand. As their eyes locked, a strange feeling came over Grace.

PART III:

DIVINE INTERVENTION

CHAPTER 9

The minute she got back to the hotel, Grace canceled her return flight to the States and hailed a taxi to the Nuovo Regina Margherita hospital.

"Please, Lord. Don't let anything happen to Tianna or her child. Put Your hands on the doctors so that they will deliver a healthy baby. I know that, in Your eyes, it is wrong to bring a child into the world to an unwed mother, but Ti and Antone were going to get married in a couple of weeks. Little Gabriella just couldn't wait."

When Grace arrived at the hospital, she found Antone pacing the floor.

"How is Ti? And the baby?"

"Tianna's in the delivery room," Antone said.

"Well, why aren't you in there with her?" Grace asked.

"I hate to see blood, and I'm afraid I wouldn't be much help," Antone answered.

"You are going in there. I will go with you, Antone, but

Tianna needs us."

When Tianna saw them enter, she lit up like a Christmas tree.

"Hi, Ti. How are you feeling, honey?" asked Grace.

"I've seen better days, but I'm really okay—considering."

As the nurses prepared Tianna for her C-section, anesthesia was being administered to Tianna through an IV. When Antone saw the needle, his face turned a shade of gray.

The senior nurse strapped Tianna's arms in a T-position to prevent her from accidentally interfering with the surgery, and a drape was placed above Ti's abdomen to keep her from seeing the incision and procedure.

Antone stood on one side of the bed holding Tianna's hand, and Grace stood behind him. When Dr. Moore began suctioning the amniotic fluid, the baby began to slowly emerge. As the head crowned, the doctor suctioned the baby's nose and mouth while slowly and methodically maneuvering its small body.

Once the baby was out, Dr. Moore asked Antone if he wanted to cut the umbilical cord. The next thing Grace saw was Antone lying on the floor as a nurse administered smelling salts to him. Grace moved to where Antone had been standing and held Tianna's hand, praising her for what a great job she was doing.

"Thank God you're here, Grace. Men are such babies," Ti said.

"I see why God made women the child bearers and not men."

As Grace cut the cord, tears flowed down her face. "This truly is a miracle from God. You just brought a new life into the world, Ti. God is so good," Grace said as she kissed her friend's head.

After the umbilical cord was cut, the nurse placed the newborn onto Tianna's breast.

"She is absolutely gorgeous. She looks just like her mama," the nurse said.

The baby had dark hair and olive skin, weighed six pounds, and was eighteen inches long.

"Welcome to the world, Gabriella Grace," said Tianna.

"What a beautiful name. What does it mean?" asked the assisting nurse.

"Gabriella means 'protected by God,' and Grace is her auntie's name," Tianna said as she looked at Grace.

"I am truly honored. I will always love and watch over you, baby girl," Grace said.

***

Categorized as "a moderate preterm," Gabrielle remained in NICI for the next two weeks, for her little lungs weren't fully developed. Originally, Gabby was supposed to stay in the ICU for at least one month, but this little girl was a fighter.

The baby was first placed on an infant warmer to keep her warm while being closely monitored, and then she was moved to an incubator.

"Gabby is quite a fighter, just like her mama," Grace told Tianna.

"Yeah, and she has her daddy's stubbornness," Ti said as she was nursing.

When Grace told Tianna about meeting the Italian producer Mattia Russo and his offer to star in his movie, Tianna screamed so loudly that Gabby jumped.

"That's great! You told him you'd do it—didn't you? I mean, it's not every day a famous movie producer offers you a part in a movie!"

"No, I didn't say yes—yet! I wanted time to think about it. You know I'm not an actress. I don't know the first thing about it."

"Well, I know you will be the best actress there is, Grace. I have all my faith in you. Please say yes. Just try it, and then you can return to the States and help me raise this wiry bundle of joy," laughed Tianna.

***

After Antone, Ti, and Gabriella left for America two weeks later, Grace called Mattia's office and arranged for a screen test.

He was happy to hear from her but upset she had waited so long to get back to him.

"*Ciao, bella.* I'm happy to hear from you, but I thought you weren't interested, for you hadn't called. We already chose someone for the part but haven't begun to shoot, so if you can come to the studio today, we will give you a try."

When he hung up the phone, Mattia was excited to once again see the woman he thought was the most beautiful woman in the world.

The screen test went better than both Mattia and Grace had ever imagined, for she was a natural. The only problem was that Grace couldn't quit staring at the handsome producer. She didn't want him to know how she felt, so she avoided eye contact the best she could.

Every time she looked at him, she felt like a giggly teenager. This was the first time in her life that anyone made her feel that way, and she didn't like it, for she felt out of control.

"Why did you wait so long to audition?" Mattia asked her.

"My best friend, who just had a baby, came to Italy to see me receive my award and went into labor three weeks early."

"Is she okay? How's the baby?"

"Thank God it all worked out, and they are safely back

home in America. I am sorry. I should have called you, but I was so concerned about Tianna and Antone that I simply forgot. She is the reason I even tried out for the role. They are the only family I have, and they mean the world to me."

"Well, then I have to meet Tianna one day and thank her," Mattia said. "You are an incredible woman and wonderful friend to take a chance of losing a once-in-a-lifetime opportunity for a friend."

"No, you don't understand, Mr. Russo. Tianna *is* the incredible woman. She is the very best friend I have, and I would do anything for her."

"Please call me Mattia," he said.

After Grace left, Mattia sat there in silence. For someone to take a chance of passing up a once-in-a-lifetime opportunity for a friend is something he couldn't comprehend. This woman was as incredibly beautiful on the inside as she was on the outside—certainly a commendable and rare trait.

***

Mattia Russo was a forty-year-old bachelor. Although he could have any woman he wanted—and he had plenty—there was something special about this particular woman that fascinated him. It wasn't that she was incredibly beautiful; there was something mysterious about her, and he wanted to know more.

Mattia was born and raised in a charming little village

called Positano. Perched along the southwestern edge of Italy, Positano is the most famous village on the Amalfi Coast.

It is known for its craggy cliffs, pastel facades, fresh seafood, maritime history, huge lemons, and ice-cold limoncello.

For centuries, the village of Positano had been known for its handmade Italian ceramics. When she was younger, Mattia's mother, Julia, made and sold ceramics in the village, and his father, Gino, was a fisherman by trade. Although the Russos were not destitute like many of the other families in the village, they were far from wealthy.

When Mattia turned twenty-one years old, his dream of becoming a movie director became a reality. Call it luck, coincidence, or a gift from God, but the first movie Mattia codirected was a box-office hit. From that day on, everything the handsome Italian touched turned to gold; thus, he became known as "the man with the golden hands."

In the nineteen years he had been directing, Mattia had taken home two Academy Awards for Best Director. He was a compassionate, generous, humble man who gave the credit for his success and wealth to his heavenly Father.

He rewarded his parents for having sacrificed everything for him by buying them a piece of property in Tuscany. The huge estate was equipped with a ten-room house, a guesthouse, and a 2,500-tree grove that harvested five thousand bottles of olives a year.

THE EVOLUTION OF GRACE

Mattia was raised Christian. Although he was wealthy, handsome, and famous, the only thing missing in Mattia's life was a godly woman who had the same old-fashioned morals and values that he did.

Granted, he had met and bedded hundreds of beautiful women. Starlets, models, and gorgeous women all tried to win the heart of the country's number one bachelor—but something was missing in every one of them.

Mattia's mother always told him, "Son, find a woman who loves God more than she loves you. That's the one to make your wife."

CHAPTER 10
Palermo, Sicily
1977

When Anna Gambino saw her granddaughter for the first time since she was born twenty-three years earlier, the woman's heart skipped several beats.

Ever since the day the family matriarch handed her daughter's newborn over to the people from the orphanage, her life was never the same.

Having to bury a child is the hardest thing a parent could ever do, but to Anna, she lost not only her daughter that day but also her granddaughter.

After Gina succumbed while giving birth, Anna walked around like a zombie. She didn't even remember attending her daughter's funeral. When Anna had a nervous breakdown and was hospitalized, she vowed that when she got out, she would find her granddaughter. She didn't care how much money it cost her—she just had to be reunited with Sophia Grace before it was too late. She owed it to her daughter, Gina.

After Gina was buried in the family mausoleum, Vito never mentioned his daughter again and said that his granddaughter was dead too.

"How can you be so horrible, Vito? We are two people who are getting old. Our only daughter is dead, and the only thing we have left in this entire world is that little baby girl our Gina gave us. God has blessed us beyond what we deserve. We are the wealthiest family in Sicily, and when we are dead, our granddaughter should be the beneficiary."

"I told you, Anna. We have *no* grandchild. When our daughter gave herself to a married man, she deserved what she got! As it says in the Bible, 'You reap what you sow.'"

"Oh, dear God. You are the devil himself! How could I have ever married such an evil man?"

From that day, Anna secretly wired her granddaughter money every month. Twenty thousand dollars a month adds up quickly, and six years later, Anna had sent Grace a total of one and a half million dollars. After all, money was no object for Anna.

After discovering Vito had been supporting not one, not two, but three mistresses, her mind was made up—if anyone should profit from the Gambino wealth and fortune, it should be their granddaughter.

Seeing Grace's picture on the cover of *Sports Illustrated* was definitely godsent, and Anna continuously thanked

Him for answering her prayers.

If she hadn't gone to town that day and walked by the newsstand seeing the words "Grace—The girl with the butterfly tattoo" on the cover, Anna may have gone the rest of her life without ever seeing Sophia again.

Anna feverishly prayed that God would soften Vito's heart so that one day he would reunite with his granddaughter too. After all, the good Lord answered her prayers once—perhaps He would do it again?

But that never happened.

Hollywood, California

Grace flew from Italy to California on Mattia's private jet.

Although she'd been on Pierre's jet many times, Mattia's was much more exquisite. It was a custom-built Global Express XRS equipped with nine cushy leather seats, aesthetically placed lighting, and many additional amenities.

A tall, voluptuous woman named Angelina was Mattia's personal flight attendant who had worked exclusively for him for three years.

As Angelina doted on Mattia, Grace had a gut feeling that the "hostess with the mostest" was more than her boss's stewardess.

As the jet flew over the famous Hollywood sign, Grace was amazed. Although she had seen many pictures, they did not do it justice.

The sign was made out of wood and sheet metal and was completed in 1923, standing 45 feet tall and 450 feet long.

Mattia told Grace the sign was originally founded in 1887 as a community for like-minded followers of the temperance movement. No one knows why they chose that name, but it may have been a reference to the area's abundant red-berried shrub, also known as California Holly.

The first Hollywood-inspired nickname dating back to 1932 was *Tollywood*, referring to the Bengali film industry in Tollygunge. Another recognized Hollywood-inspired nickname is *Bollywood*.

It was the early 1930s when Los Angeles Times publisher Harry Chandler decided to invest in an upscale real-estate development called Hollywoodland, which capitalized on the growing recognition of Hollywood as a movie industry mecca.

Chandler and his partners invested twenty-one thousand dollars for forty-five-foot-high white block letters that were anchored to telephone poles and illuminated by four thousand light bulbs.

Although the sign symbolizes glamour and stardom, it also represents broken dreams. In 1932, stage actress Peg Entwistle moved from New York to Los Angeles to try her luck in the movies. Soon after, Entwhistle received a part in a murder mystery film, but when the studio did not renew the option on her contract upon its completion, the twenty-four-year-old wannabe starlet climbed a ladder to the "H" on the sign and jumped to her death.

"Oh no! How sad. Thanks for telling me, but there are too many similarities here for my liking. I'm gonna be twenty-four years old on my next birthday; I also moved from New York to Los Angeles, and I am trying my luck in the movie business too. I sure hope my ending is not like Entwistle's."

When the jet landed, Mattia had his limousine waiting there for them. After disembarking, Mattia gave Grace a private tour of the city. Although the flight from Italy to LA took a little over five hours, Grace wasn't tired, for she managed to get a catnap in and was raring to go.

Hollywood was "tourist central," for the sidewalks were packed with sightseers and locals shopping in the designer stores, curiously wanting to see what all the buzz was about.

Many notable movie factories such as Columbia Pictures, Walt Disney Studios, Paramount Pictures, Warner Bros. and Universal Pictures call Hollywood home.

Paramount Pictures was going to produce *A Woman of God*.

Paramount was the sixth-oldest film studio in the United States that introduced such superstars as Clara Bow, Gloria Swanson, Rudolph Valentino, and Veronica Lake, among others.

Paramount Pictures was also the founding father of the animation films *Popeye* and *Mickey Mouse*, so Grace figured if it was good enough for Mickey, it was good enough for her.

Buses flooded the streets with tourists who wanted to get a glimpse of celebrities, celebrity homes, glamorous hotels, celebrity hangouts, the Chinese Theatre, the Hollywood Walk of Fame, and the Dolby Theater.

As she was walking down the street, Grace spotted one

of her all-time favorite actors, Robert Redford. The scrappy blonde man was even more handsome in person than in the movies.

As she was starstruck and speechless, Mattia laughed at her enthusiasm. In his Italian accent, he said, "*Bella*, I hope you like Hollywood, for we will most likely be here for the next two years."

"Two years! I can't be away from my dog Max, Tianna, Antone, and little Gabby that long!"

"My delicate flower, perhaps they can visit you? And remember, I can always fly you on my plane there if needed."

When Grace settled into her posh suite, she immediately called her best friend. "Tianna, I just landed in Hollywood. You should see it! How's Max? How's Antone, and how's my little godchild?"

"Slow down, girlie. Max is fine. Antone is busy working overtime to help us make it on one income now, and Gabriella is not so little anymore. She is growing like a weed.

Gabby goo-goos all day long and loves Max. That's something I wanted to talk to you about, Grace. Since you are going to be over there that long, don't you think it's better if we keep Max with us? He's getting older and sleeps a lot. We really love him, and Gabby is crazy about him."

Grace was silent as tears welled up in her eyes,

threatening to fall on her Versace silk suit.

"You're probably right, but I don't know how I'm gonna be away from him that long."

So it was final. Max would remain in New York with her friends until the movie was finished.

***

For the next two years, Grace and Mattia were together twenty-four seven, working side by side on the movie: spending most of the day at the studio and, afterward, they would grab a bite.

Mattia leased two fully equipped penthouse suites in the Waldorf Astoria Beverly Hills equipped with all the modern-day amenities, and Grace didn't need a car, for Mattia's limo was on call whenever she needed it.

When Grace told her old boss, Pierre Devereaux, she was taking a hiatus from modeling to star in a movie, he was not a happy camper.

"A hiatus? You are not getting any younger, honey. Beautiful new faces walk in that door every day, and people want to see fresh, young girls. The younger, the better."

After five years working at Lancomer, Grace thought Pierre would've been a little more upset to see her go, and she couldn't forget what Mrs. Devereaux once told her about: after the age of twenty-five, a model is considered old.

Grace was falling hard for Mattia, and to her surprise,

she discovered the feeling was mutual. Outside of a peck on the cheek, Mattia never made any advances on his starlet. It had always been work and no play. She assumed Mattia was seeing other women, but she felt it was none of her business and never brought the subject up.

One day, Grace called Tianna and confided in her best friend about the deep feelings she had for Mattia.

"*What*? That's wonderful! The handsome Italian must be really good in the sack to have Grace Antonelli's heart! I mean, it's about time! You're twenty-four years old and have never been intimate with a man. I respect you, Grace—I really do—but you are way overdue! Maybe he is *the one*, and little Gabby will have a baby cousin to play with soon."

"I hate to disappoint you, Ti, but we have never had sex. I'm not saying I don't want to, but Mattia has never even kissed me. I'm starting to think something is wrong with me."

"*Nothing's* wrong with you. You are dubbed the world's new Sophia Loren, and every man wants to be with you, and every woman wants to *be* you. Maybe Mattia's just shy and doesn't want to make the first move," Tianna said.

"Or maybe he's into men. You never know these days with these gorgeous guys today—like our hairdresser, Santiago. I was floored when he came out of the closet. I had the biggest crush on that Latin hunk, and when I saw him holding that young stud's hand, I almost fainted! I mean—what a waste!" Tianna laughed.

"Oh no, Ti! I would bet my life Mattia is only into women. And as far as Santiago, I guess he prefers men to women. I never understood that kind of thing, but I guess everyone has different tastes. The world is so crazy; the times are changing, and so are people. Whenever I see two people of the same sex in an inappropriate manner, I remember Leviticus 20:13, 'You shall not lie with a male as with a woman! It's an abomination to God.'"

When Tianna hung up the phone, Grace thought about what her friend said. That night, when Grace said her prayers, she asked God to guide her on what to do.

Although deep down inside she wanted to be more intimate with Mattia, Grace would never think of having sex with him or anyone else until she was married. And once Mattia discovered Grace was an inexperienced virgin, he probably wouldn't want her. But she had made a vow to God that she would never be with a man until she had a wedding ring on her finger, and one thing Grace Antonelli discovered the hard way was you *never* disobey the Lord, for if you do, you will surely pay the consequences. As it says in Galatians 6:7, "For whatsoever a man soweth, that shall he also reap."

CHAPTER 11

The filming of *A Woman of God* was almost complete. The cast was taking a month's hiatus before resuming, so Grace flew to New York while Mattia returned to Italy to spend time with his ailing mother.

When Grace walked into Ti's apartment, Max was waiting there to welcome his mommy with a thousand kisses. Although he was thrilled to see her, he remained close to Gabby.

Grace felt slightly rejected, and her face said it all. Tianna walked over to Grace and put her arm around her.

"Honey, don't be sad. Max is happy to see you. He has gotten extremely close to Gabriella and thinks his job now is to protect her. They are so cute together, but he will always be *your* baby. We are just his surrogate family."

Although she was a bit sad, Grace was at peace knowing how happy Max was. She saw how much her friends loved him, and with her crazy schedule the way it had been lately, he was better off with them than with her.

Gabby was now two years old and becoming quite a handful. When she saw Grace walk into the room, she muttered, "Aunt Gwace."

The whole time Grace was away making the movie, Tianna showed her daughter pictures of Grace and FaceTimed her so Gabby would know who she was.

Gabby was a beautiful baby who had her mama's exotic looks and her papa's sweet personality.

"I'm so glad you are finally here. However long you are staying in New York, you will stay with us. I know our apartment is not very big, but we will manage."

When Grace moved to Los Angeles, she sold her New York apartment, so for the time being, she had no place to call her own. Although Tianna and Antone's place was small, it was comfy, and Grace wouldn't want to be anywhere else.

For the next two weeks, Grace and Tianna caught up on girly talk. Antone was still working at Lancomer and was busy doing double shifts for more income.

"I hate to see Antone work so hard. He looks so tired, Ti."

"Yes, he's tired, but we really need the money. We have been living off of my savings, which, thank God, I had. During the years I modeled, I was lucky to sock away a couple hundred thousand dollars, but New York is soooooo expensive. Our rent alone is five thousand dollars a month."

"Why don't you buy a small house outside the city? I'd be glad to help you guys. After all, you are the only family I have, and Gabby is my 'surrogate daughter,'" laughed Grace.

"You always wanted to live on a farm with horses. Let's go look at some places while I'm here. We can look at Cherry Valley, which is not that far from the city so Antone wouldn't have that far to drive every day. Gabby can have a pony, and Max will have land to live out his golden doggy years."

"We really can't afford it, Grace, but it doesn't cost anything to go and look, I guess."

So, the next day, Grace secretly called a realtor friend in New York and told her what she was looking for. The realtor sent Grace a list of several places that had land with a house—some even had a small barn. Grace, Tianna, Gabby, and Max took a ride the next morning; unbeknownst to Ti, Grace had something up her sleeve.

When they arrived at the first address the realtor gave, Tianna was speechless. Nestled on ten acres of land was a log cabin house next to a six-stall barn with a fresh stream that ran through the property.

The house, originally built in 1848, had four bedrooms and two bathrooms but was recently updated with all the modern-day amenities. Off the main bedroom was a huge Jacuzzi tub and shower that could easily accommodate four people, and there was a huge fenced-in yard for Gabby and

Max. It was located at 123 Heaven Lane on a cul-de-sac, so there would be little traffic, which would be great for Max and Gabby.

"Heaven Lane? What a wonderful name for a street," Tianna said.

When Grace opened the car door, Max jumped out and ran. Gabby tried to keep up with him, but her little legs were not fast enough. She would get frustrated and yell, "Maxie! Wait for Gabby!"

"Holy Mary—Mother of God. This place is beautiful. But why are we here? I can't afford this place. We might be able to afford the barn, but that's it," laughed Tianna.

Grace opened the front door with the key she retrieved from the lockbox. As soon as Gabby and Max got inside, they resumed chasing one another.

"This is lovely, Grace. It is my dream home, but it's just that—a dream."

For the next week, all Tianna could do was talk about the house on Heaven Lane. The two women looked at three other homes after leaving Heaven Lane, but it was useless, for they couldn't compare to the log cabin. When asked the price, the realtor told Grace the owner was asking $750,000 but possibly would come down a bit.

One morning, Grace discovered Antone in the kitchen having coffee before leaving for work. Tianna and Gabby were still asleep so this was the first time Grace had been alone with her long-time friend since she arrived.

Looking perplexed, she asked Antone, "What's wrong, my friend? Is everything okay with you and Ti? I know I haven't talked to you in a while, but you guys are always on my mind. I hope you are happy. You have such a wonderful family, and I want to think I had something to do with it."

"Of course we are happy, and yes, Grace, it is all because of you. I never thought I could love anyone like I love Ti and Gabby. I just wish I could afford to buy them that house. Ti *loves* it, and what a great place it would be to raise our child. But I just can't swing it."

Every night they were apart, Mattia FaceTimed Grace. They would discuss what they had been doing, but mostly, Mattia would talk about his mother. It was obvious that the mother/son relationship was very strong. Mattia's father had died two years earlier, and since Mattia was away so much, his mother was left alone.

One night, while they were FaceTiming, Mattia introduced Grace to his mother, Julia. The eighty-year-old attractive woman told Grace, "I would love to meet you one day. My Mattia speaks so highly of you."

When Mattia got back on the phone, he said, "Grace, I just received a new script for a movie. It's fantastic, and I think you would be great for the part. The story is about a beautiful madam who falls for a much younger man who is studying to be a priest.

It will be filmed in Mykonos, Greece, but first, I want to visit my ranch in Montana—God's country. It's in

Missoula, and we can stay there. I know you will love it."

"Montana! I've always wanted to go there. Thanks for thinking of me for the role, but I don't think I could play a prostitute. I would be horrible in that role. And I didn't know you had property in Montana."

"Yes, I own a small ranch, which I never get to go to and enjoy. There's fly-fishing, horseback riding and lots of animals. It is my 'therapy place'—the place I go to when I need peace and to be alone."

"The only place I love more than Montana is Africa. Three years ago, I purchased a huge piece of undeveloped land located in Togo. It's fifty acres of preserved land where the animals run freely, and there is no hunting or killing allowed."

"I absolutely *love* Africa. I always said if I had the means, I would live there."

"Who knows what the future holds?" he smiled.

Grace knew that Mattia was a world hunter who made yearly hunting trips to Togo to feed the starving children there. Although Grace was against killing animals, if they were slain to feed the hungry children, then she could accept it.

"Please say yes, Grace. I can fly to New York this week and show you the script. I've never been to New York at Christmas time, and I wouldn't want to see it with anyone but you."

Just the thought of seeing Mattia again brought back the butterflies in her stomach, and to have him with her and her friends during Christmas was a dream come true.

"Oh, I'd like that very much. Let me know when you'll be arriving. And tell your mother I hope to meet her someday."

"Good night, Grace. Oh, believe me, you will be meeting Mama sooner than you think. I'll be in touch soon. *Ciao, bellissima.*"

As Grace started to say goodbye, she noticed a sultry brunette walk up behind Mattia and run her fingers through his thick, curly hair. When Grace saw the woman, she was unable to speak.

"Grace, are you still there? Mattia asked, but there was no one on the other end.

When Grace hung up the phone, she threw herself down on the bed as a river of tears flowed from her eyes.

***

When Tianna heard Grace crying, she knocked on the door. "Gracie, are you okay? Can I come in?"

Trembling, Grace answered, "Come on in, Ti, but I don't want Gabby to see me this way."

When Ti walked into the room, her heart broke, for the entire time the two girls had been friends, she had never seen Grace cry. Grace was definitely the tougher one of the two.

Grace Antonelli had been through a lot in her life. She never knew who her parents were or the reason they gave her up. Then, her adoptive parents died suddenly, leaving her alone when she was seventeen years old.

Grace was the kindest, most compassionate, loving woman Tianna had ever met, and she deserved nothing but happiness.

"What's wrong, honey?" Ti asked, hugging Grace.

"I just talked to Mattia. He asked if I'd star in another movie that is going to be filmed in Greece and said he would fly to New York next week so that I could look over the script."

"That's wonderful, Grace. Finally, I will get to meet the mystery man! I can't wait. You should be thrilled, so why are you crying?"

"Because when he (sob) was saying goodbye (sob), a gorgeous woman walked behind him and began rubbing his head (sob sob)."

"Maybe she was his sister? Don't jump to conclusions just yet."

"He doesn't have a sister!" Grace screamed.

"Ah, oh. I think our Gracie has finally fallen in love," Tianna said.

CHAPTER 12

Mattia flew to New York on his private jet and booked the penthouse suite at the Mandarin Oriental for one week. The high-end hotel cost thirty-six thousand dollars a night, but wherever Mattia went, he went first class.

The five-star hotel was designed to exude the Manhattan experience, and each private suite had a wraparound view of Central Park and the Manhattan skyline. Many celebrities stayed there when they were in the city, such as Tom Hanks, Jack Nicholson and Robert De Niro.

When Mattia told Grace he was coming in on December 23, she couldn't sleep for days.

"Let's go to the city tomorrow and buy something that will knock Mattia's socks off," Tianna said. "And let's book a hair appointment at Vidal Sassoon Salon and have Mr. Vidal give you a new look."

"What's wrong with the way I look?" Grace asked.

"Nothing at all. There isn't a woman on this planet that doesn't want to look like you, honey. It's just that getting a new look can be the perfect excuse to try something outside of your comfort zone."

The next day, the two women took a taxi to the city, leaving Max and Gabby with Antone. Their first stop: Vidal Sassoon on Madison Avenue. As Grace entered the salon, the room went silent.

Vidals' personal assistant, Mika, took the two women to a room in the back so that they didn't disrupt the other customers. In his Cockney accent, Vidal Sassoon said, "My God, Ms. Antonelli. You are more beautiful in person than you are on the big screen."

The English stylist immediately began cutting Grace's long hair into the geometric cut he had become famous for. When he was finished, Grace looked elegant yet sultry, as her hair was shorter in the back and longer on the sides. While Vidal was cutting Grace's hair, he noticed the butterfly tattoo on her back.

"I absolutely *love* your tattoo. I remember when you did the *Sports Illustrated* cover, and the media began calling you 'the girl with the butterfly tattoo.' But this doesn't look like an ink tattoo."

"It's not Mr. Sassoon. It was something I was born with."

After looking at it more closely, Vidal made the sign of the cross. "You are a very lucky woman, Ms. Antonelli. God certainly has blessed you."

When he was finished, Vidal took Grace by the arm and

walked her into the main salon. "Ladies, look at my newest creation. I call it 'The Graceful Butterfly.'"

Thierry Mugler and Versace boutiques were both within walking distance from the salon, and the very first outfit Grace tried on in Mugler, she bought it. It was a black clingy jumpsuit adorned with real mink on the cuffs and neckline.

When she stepped out of the dressing room, the salesgirl gasped. "You look gorgeous! That outfit was made for you, ma'am. You could be a model."

Grace and Tianna looked at each other and laughed.

"She doesn't know you *are* one of the most famous models in the world, Grace. What planet has she been living on?"

***

The next afternoon, Grace hailed a cab to the Mandarin Oriental. She was nervous to see Mattia but tried not to show it. As she walked into the lobby, everyone stared. She spotted Mattia sitting at the bar, having a glass of wine and having a conversation with the bartender. When Grace entered, the server shut up.

Mattia turned to see what the man was gawking at. When he saw Grace, he began choking on the wine. The bartender ran to Mattia and patted him on the back.

"Are you okay, Mr. Russo?"

"Honey, are you okay?" Grace asked.

"Yes, I'm fine. When I saw the most beautiful woman in the world walk into the room, I choked on my wine."

Grace looked around to see who Mattia was talking about, thinking perhaps Penelope Cruz or Sharon Stone might have just walked in.

Mattia laughed so hard he had tears in his eyes. "Grace, I was talking about you, honey! That's what I love about you. You are humble and kind and don't know how beautiful you really are."

The next day, Grace and Mattia went to the Empire State Building and the Rockefeller Plaza. It was under the big Christmas tree at the Plaza when it happened.

After sightseeing for hours, Grace's feet were hurting, and she told Mattia she wanted to sit down. It had just begun to snow, and as the snowflakes landed on Grace's nose, Mattia began kissing them off, working his way down to her mouth. As their lips touched... *Fireworks! Fireworks! Fireworks!*

Everything around Grace began spinning, and if she hadn't been sitting down, she knew she would have fallen. She always dreamt what it would be like to kiss someone you were in love with—and to her surprise, it was even better!

***

Early Christmas morning, Mattia arrived at Antone and Tianna's with a sack full of wrapped presents. When Gabby opened hers, she squealed so loud that Max ran and hid under the bed.

Grace bought Mattia a Louis Vuitton alligator briefcase for his Christmas present. She wasn't sure if he would like it but what do you buy someone who has two of everything already?

Thankfully, he loved it and thanked Grace over and over before handing her a small package from Cartier. Inside the box was a diamond Ballon Bleu de Cartier watch.

"What? Why? This is way too much!" said Grace.

"I heard you talking about wanting that watch, so here it is. Nothing but the best for you, my love."

Mattia grabbed Grace and kissed her longer and harder than he had ever before.

"*Ti amo, bellisima.*"

After everyone exchanged presents, Grace handed Tianna a small envelope. "What is this? You have given me enough. Your friendship is all I ever wanted. Since the first time I threw a glass of champagne on you, I've always admired and looked up to you," laughed Tianna.

"You are truly one of a kind, Gracie. When the Lord created you, He threw away the mold, for there is no one on earth as good, pure, and *real* as you, my friend."

When Tianna opened the envelope, a set of keys fell on

the floor.

"What the heck is this?" Tianna asked Grace.

"These are the keys to you and Antone's new house. You are now the proud owners of the log cabin located at 123 Heaven Lane. It is paid in full, so you don't have to worry about a mortgage or anything else. This is where little Gabby can grow up, and my Max will live out his years running free."

"*What? No way!* This is way too much, Grace. I can't allow it," Ti said.

After several minutes of complete silence, Antone said, "If we do accept, I promise we will pay you back every dime. It might take a lifetime, but you'll get paid back every cent."

"Absolutely not! I love you both very much, and you are the only family I have left. You know I can afford it, and whenever I need to get away from it all, it'll be my refuge."

They hugged as they cried with happiness. Grace felt so good to be able to make her best friends' dream come true.

Grace Antonelli had always been a giver. One of her favorite sayings was James 1:17—"Every good gift and every perfect gift is from above, and cometh down from the Father of lights, with whom is no variableness, neither shadow of turning."

Grace had earned millions of dollars during her

modeling career, and the twenty-thousand-dollar monthly direct deposit that came from an anonymous sender had accumulated to almost a couple of million dollars. She still had no idea who the remitter was, and until she did, she would not touch the money.

Palermo, Italy
1981

When Anna Gambino received the news about her husband, she was shocked. Vito had been diagnosed with bone cancer and given three years max to live.

Anna had mixed feelings, for although she had succumbed to many years of abuse from him, Anna was a Christian who lived her life by God's teaching. The Lord preached to forgive others because He forgave us so generously, so compassionately, and so undeservedly. God forgave man with compassion and love, and man should do the same, so when Vito was told he had only a few years to live, Anna put aside her contempt for him.

Anna Gambino wasn't a mean or hateful woman; on the contrary, she was the sweetest, most caring woman who was loved by everyone. When the seventeen-year-old girl was forced to marry Vito in a "made marriage," Anna wasn't in love with him. In fact, she married a complete stranger for she knew nothing about him except he was powerful and wealthy, and whatever Vito Gambino wanted, he got!

After discovering Vito was the one responsible for giving the orders to have people killed, she was devastated. Every night, Anna prayed for God to soften Vito's cold heart and change him, for if anyone could do that—her God could.

By marrying Vito, her parents would never have to

worry about having food on the table, and divorce was something that was not in the cards. To Anna, marriage had a divine meaning, and when Anna said, "I do," it was till death do them part.

Although Vito provided Anna with a life of wealth, the one thing missing was love.

As the years went by, Anna grew to love her husband the best that she could and be content with her life—that was, up until the death of their only child, Gina.

On the day their daughter died giving birth to their grandchild, a piece of Anna also died. Losing her daughter and then having her grandchild sent away to an adoption agency in America had taken a toll on the Gambino matriarch.

From the day baby Grace was taken, Vito and Anna had a loveless marriage. Anna quickly learned to close her eyes to Vito's sordid affairs and quit having sex with him. All Anna wanted was to wait until God called her home so she could be reunited with her precious daughter, Gina, but in the meantime, as long as she remained on earth, Anna Gambino had one goal—to be reunited and take care of her granddaughter, Sophia Grace.

CHAPTER 13

Grace Antonelli had never been happier in her entire life. It felt so good to have the means to buy the ranch for her friends, Antone and Tianna. Little Gabriella and Max would have a beautiful place to play and grow up on, and Grace knew how much her dog loved little Gabby, so she told Tianna, "We will share joint custody of our boy Max."

The five days that Mattia stayed in New York, the couple was inseparable. It was the night before he flew back to Hollywood when he told Grace he was falling in love with her.

She said she felt the same way but was concerned about the woman she saw on the FaceTime call.

"But what about the beautiful woman who was with you and your mom that day?"

Mattia laughed. "Grace, that was Viviana. She is my oldest childhood friend. She is like my sister. She was there that day checking on my mother for me. I love her like a sister—that's all. It is *you* who has won my heart."

Before Mattia left, Grace told him she would try out for the part in his next movie. "That's great, honey, but there's no need to try out—you already have the part!" he said as he passionately kissed her. Although, at times, they had been intertwined in heavy make-out sessions, they never crossed the line. At first, Grace was afraid that her view of not having sex before marriage would have Mattia running for the hills, but when she discovered he not only agreed but respected her all the more, she was relieved.

"I'd like you to come to my ranch in Montana next week. My mother will be there, and she really wants to meet you, honey. I'll send the jet to get you. It's really cold there now and snowing, but I will keep you warm."

***

Saying goodbye to Max, Gabby, Antone, and Ti was harder than Grace thought it would be. "Gracie, I'm so happy for you, honey. Mattia is wonderful, and he really loves you. I'm glad you agreed to do his new movie, and going to Greece to film it is the icing on the cake. Have fun in Montana, and good luck with his mom."

The following week, Mattia sent his jet for Grace to fly her to the ranch. At first, she was sad he wasn't on the plane, but he told her something very important to do and would see her soon.

As the limo drove through the main gates of the ranch, Grace noticed elk, bears, and bobcats in the fields.

"Oh my. Is it dangerous here?" Grace asked the driver.

Laughing, he said, "Remember, the danger that is most to be feared is never the danger we are most afraid of. This is home to these animals—we are the visitors. Be cautious, but you have no worries, for Mr. Russo will protect you."

As the limo drove up to the main house, Grace thought she must have died and gone to heaven, for she had never before seen anything as magnificent as the ranch. It was absolutely God's country.

Situated on the 750 acres were several magnificent guesthouses. The groundskeeper lived in the one next to a huge barn that housed six champion thoroughbred horses and a ten thousand square foot log cabin mansion.

Waiting by the door was Mattia with the million-dollar smile that made Grace's heart skip beats, and next to him was a little Italian woman who she knew was his mother.

"Mama, this is my future wife, Grace. Your daughter-in-law-to-be who will be the mother of your grandchildren."

Grace stood there, unable to speak. First, she wasn't sure if he was just saying these things or if it was his way of asking her to marry him. But she didn't need to wait any longer, for Mattia got down on his knee and pulled out a huge diamond ring.

"Grace Antonelli—the love of my life and the woman I have been waiting for all of my life—will you marry me?"

***

THE EVOLUTION OF GRACE

At first, Grace thought she must be dreaming, for she had dreamt of this moment many times. She stood there, not being able to answer at first. "Grace—will you make me the happiest man on earth and become my wife?" Mattia asked again.

"Of course I'll marry you, honey. I have been praying to God to send me the man He chose for me, and He sent you!"

After Mattia and Grace embraced, his mother hugged Grace.

"You have made my son the happiest man on earth, Grace. Thank You, God, for this blessing."

Grace immediately called Tianna and told her the news.

"Mattia just asked me to be his wife! I'm still in shock and would think it is all a dream except on my finger is a big, brilliant diamond ring."

"*Yay!* Can I be your maid of honor, and Gabby be the flower girl?"

"Of course. And Max will be included as Gabby can walk him down the aisle on his leash."

"So, when is this royal wedding taking place and where?" asked Tianna.

"We haven't got to that part yet. We will have to wait until *A Woman of God* is finished. I'm not sure if we will get married before we start filming the next movie or wait until it's finished."

"No! You simply cannot wait that long. How long can this man wait to make it right? My little Grace will finally know what it's like to make love to the man she adores."

"Whoa, Nelly! Thank God Mattia is on the same page as me when it comes to that. We both agreed to wait until our honeymoon night."

"But he is a man with needs," Tianna said. "You don't want him to stray, do you?"

"I have faith and trust him. He knows how I feel about premarital sex and feels the same. He said he is blessed to be marrying a woman who has never been with a man in that way."

"Well, then it's done. Do you want to fly here so we can celebrate? We all really miss you," Ti said.

"I'd love to, Ti, but we have a few more weeks before finishing *A Woman of God*, and then I will have more time. I'll let you know as soon as we set a date. You can help design my dress and help with all the other arrangements. I love you, Ti. Give everyone a kiss from me," Grace said as she hung up the phone.

***

That night, Mattia and Grace decided on a wedding date. They would get married on Grace's birthday, July 4, 1982. Grace would be twenty-eight years old, and Mattia would be forty-four.

Grace immediately put Tianna in charge of making all the arrangements for the wedding since she was extremely busy wrapping up the movie.

The ceremony was going to be held on Mattia's ranch, and the couple would be driven in a two-horse carriage steered by Mattia's two favorite horses, ironically named Romeo and Juliet.

When the movie was finished, word in the industry was *A Woman of God* was sure to be nominated for an Academy Award.

"Honey, I have to fly to Athens to meet with Franco Gagliardi, the movie producer. He wants to discuss the new movie and said this would be my best film yet.

It'll only be a week, so I'll meet you at the awards ceremony. I'll get there as quickly as I can, for I want to be there when they call your name for Best Actress."

"Don't put the cart before the horse, babe. Meryl Streep is up for her role in *Anything Goes*, and she's hard to beat. I'm just blessed and honored to have been nominated. And *you* have been nominated for Best Producer. Wouldn't it be something if we both brought home an Oscar statuette?" Grace asked.

***

As the day of the Academy Awards neared, Grace was a nervous wreck. Not only was she up for an Academy Award, but her wedding to Mattia was quickly approaching.

Thank God for Tianna, for she had taken care of all the arrangements, from the seating to hiring the best caterer in the world. The only thing left was to find the perfect wedding dress, so Grace made an appointment with Vera Kimu, the designer to the celebrities, for the day after the award banquet.

The day of the Academy Awards arrived. As Grace was getting ready to go to the Roosevelt Hotel in Los Angeles—the venue where the Academy Awards would be held that year—her phone rang.

"Hi, *bella*. I just boarded the jet. I should be there in a few hours, so don't fret. The weather is not the greatest, but I will be there. I want to see my love win the Oscar."

"What about you?—You are the best director, and word is you will win, my love," Grace said. "And if the weather is too bad, *please* don't fly. Although I really want you here, your life is more important than any trophy."

"Absolutely no! *You* are more important than anything in my life, and I wouldn't miss it for the world."

As the hours went by and there was no word from Mattia, Grace became more anxious. When she tried calling him, it went straight to his voicemail.

"*Ciao*. This is Mattia. Please leave a message, and I will return the call as quickly as I can." Just hearing the sound of his voice brought those butterflies back.

Grace wore a black Versace gown that Donatella designed just for her. It had a long sleeve on one side while

THE EVOLUTION OF GRACE

the other was sleeveless, showing off her famous butterfly tattoo.

Accessories were simple but elegant, as Cartier loaned Grace their finest chandelier diamond earrings and diamond cuff.

When she stepped out of the limo, the crowd went wild with the fans screaming, "Grace, Grace, Grace! The girl with the butterfly tattoo."

As the celebrities strutted down the red carpet in their designer gowns and tuxes, stopping to pose for a photo, Grace had to pinch herself to make sure she wasn't dreaming.

Grace Antonelli, the orphaned baby that nobody wanted was at the Oscars being nominated for Best Actress. The only thing missing was her love, Mattia.

Where are you? Why aren't you here, honey? she said to herself when, out of nowhere, a butterfly appeared and landed on Grace's shoulder. But unlike the other beautiful butterflies that flew on her before, this one was not colorful but almost completely black. She froze in fear, for she knew something was terribly wrong.

"Ms. Antonelli, please smile. You look like you've just seen a ghost," a photographer said.

For a minute, Grace couldn't move, for she knew something was about to happen or had already happened. The first time it happened was when Uncle Ben molested her. The second time, she was boarding a plane and had to deplane to go back home and get something she had forgotten. The plane crashed an hour later, killing everyone on it, and the next time was the night her parents were killed in an accident.

As the photographer walked over to shoo the insect away, Grace said, "No, don't touch it. Leave it alone. If you need to take a picture, take it with the butterfly. It isn't harming anything."

After dozens of photos were taken, Grace was escorted to the front row, hoping to see Mattia waiting there. After making numerous attempts to call him, she was now frantic.

"Lord, please don't let anything be wrong with Mattia. I beg of you," she prayed as the emcee announced—"And the winner for Best Actress is Grace Antonelli."

The entire room stood on their feet and clapped. As Grace walked to the stage, her phone rang. It had been set on silent so it went directly to voice mail.

As she gave her acceptance speech, her voice was shaky.

"As a little girl, all I ever wanted was to be a movie star. I used to go to the movie theater and watch the beautiful actresses kiss the handsome men. When I was born, my parents didn't want me, and they gave me away."

Oohs and aahs came from the audience.

"My adoptive parents were the most wonderful people who showered me with love. Sadly, they were killed in a car accident several years ago, and they never got to see my success as a fashion model or actress. My fiancé, director Mattia Russo, who just took home Best Director for the film *A Woman of God*, is absent tonight, but I want to tell him, "Thank you, my love, for having faith in me and showing me what love really is. I also want to thank my best friends, Tianna and Antone, and my dog Max for their unconditional love, but most of all, I want to thank my heavenly Father for none of this would have happened if it wasn't for Him."

When Grace finished her acceptance speech, she got a standing ovation. Everyone was clapping while some of them had tears in their eyes.

Grace returned to her seat to find her phone blinking, informing her she had a message. It was from Mattia's mother. Between the noise and Mrs. Russo's strong Italian accent, Grace could barely understand what she was saying.

The only thing she remembered hearing was Mrs. Russo say, "Grace! My boy, Mattia, was in a terrible accident. His plane fell down in the storm and crashed. Mattia's *dead*! My Mattia is gone!" as she fell to the floor.

PART IV:

SWEET REDEMPTION

CHAPTER 14

When Grace came to, she had no idea where she was. Lying on a strange bed with her arms strapped down and a woman dressed in white checking her vitals, Grace assumed she was in a hospital. But why was she there, and how did she get there?

Grace Antonelli, the world's most famous actress who just won Best Actress, was at the Mayo Clinic in Arizona.

"Hi, honey. I've been so worried about you. I got here as soon as they called me. You've been asleep for weeks now, and I have been worried sick about you," Tianna said.

"Who are you? Where am I?" Grace asked as she tried loosening her arms. She was conscious only for a moment before she fell back into a deep sleep.

"Why doesn't she know me, and why are her arms tied down?" cried Tianna.

A doctor walked into the room and introduced himself as Grace's physician, Dr. Williams.

"Why doesn't Grace know me?" Tianna asked the doctor. "What's happening to her?"

"Grace has had a mild breakdown. When she passed out, she hit her head on the cement, causing amnesia, and was flown here from California, for they felt this was the best place for her."

"Who gave that order? Who are *they*? I'm her closest friend, and she has no one else," asked Tianna.

"Ma'am, I'm not at liberty to divulge that information. But this is where they wanted Ms. Antonelli to be admitted, and quite frankly, I'm glad they did. Miss Antonelli is very, very sick, and we have the best psychiatrists in the world here."

"I'm going to ask you one more time—*Who* wanted Grace sent here?" Tianna asked again more sternly.

"All I can say is it's a woman claiming she is Sophia's next of kin. She is handling all the details and taking care of any bills," the doctor said.

"Next of kin! But that's impossible. Her parents are deceased, and she has no relatives. What was the woman's name? What did she look like? And her name is Grace—not Sophia!"

After the doctor left the room, Tianna held Grace's hands and cried.

"Honey, please get better. I don't know what's going on here, but we need you. Max and Gabrielle miss you so much."

***

After Grace collapsed at the awards ceremony, it was world-breaking news. CNN flashed across the television screen—"Grace Antonelli, the girl with the butterfly tattoo, remains in a semicoma at the Mayo Clinic in Arizona. After winning the Oscar for Best Actress in the movie *A Woman of God*, Ms. Antonelli discovered her fiancé, director Mattia Russo's private jet crashed, killing him instantly."

When Anna Gambino heard what happened, she immediately flew to Los Angeles with all the appropriate documents proving that Grace was her biological granddaughter and she was the next of kin.

When Anna walked into the ICU, her heart broke. Although she hadn't seen her granddaughter since the day she was born, Anna loved her more than anything in the world.

Vito—Anna's husband and Grace's grandfather—remained back at the Gambino compound in Palermo, slowly withering away from cancer. He was no longer the strong, powerful don who ruled his Mafia family; instead, he was now a frail, pathetic old man.

The matriarch of the Gambino family sat by Grace's bed twenty-four-seven, holding her hand while she prayed to God for His healing. "Heavenly Father, I lost Sophia Grace once—please don't take her away from me again."

***

Tianna rushed to the hospital as soon as they called her. When she walked in and saw Anna by Grace's bed, she stopped. The woman could be Grace's twin in about forty years, for the resemblance was uncanny.

The woman's dark hair with grey strands was rolled in a tight bun, and her eyes were shaped exactly like Grace's but much darker. After Anna explained to Tianna what had happened in Palermo years earlier, Tianna broke down in tears.

"Poor Grace. I mean Sophia. She always wondered who her parents were and why they gave her away. I pray she gets better and gets to meet you. She is the most beautiful and loving person in the world."

When Grace arrived at Mayo Clinic, she was immediately put in a medically induced coma to help reduce the risk of a brain injury, for when she passed out, she hit her head on the floor, causing her brain to swell.

By reducing the electrical activity in the brain and slowing down the brain's metabolism, an induced coma can minimize the swelling and inflammation of the brain.

"How long will she be like this doctor?" Anna asked.

"That depends on Sophia. In most cases, a coma is induced for a few days to a few weeks. It will depend on how she comes along—we will have to wait and see. Of course, the longer she remains in a coma, the possibility of risks increases, for there is an increased risk of infection, but the procedure has improved considerably in recent years due to the advances in monitoring technology. All we can do now is wait and pray."

***

Over the next few weeks, Grace would periodically wake up for a few minutes each day, questioning her whereabouts and who the woman was by her side. The doctor was pleased that Grace still had mental and physical skills but was concerned about why she still had amnesia. Usually, when a person has amnestic syndrome, they usually know who they are, but Grace didn't. She had no recollection of what happened to her, who she was, and how she got there. Diagnosed with retrograde amnesia, Grace was unable to remember events from her past.

The damage to the memory-making part of her brain—the thalamus—caused short-term memory loss. Dr. Williams said there was no treatment to cure amnesia, and they would concentrate on condition management, such as occupational therapy, memory training, and vitamin B1 supplements.

A few months later, when Grace began showing signs of improvement, she was moved to the psychiatric department, where she would engage in daily occupational therapy and psychotherapy.

Anna never returned to Palermo, vowing to stay with her granddaughter until she completely recovered, or for some reason, if Grace never returned to normalcy, Anna would bring her back to Italy to care for her.

That night, while Anna said her prayers, she thanked God for helping her reunite with Grace.

"Father in heaven, thank You for helping me find my granddaughter. I realize she doesn't know who I am yet, but this is an opportunity for her to get to know me. Through me, Sophia Grace will learn the truth about why she was given up for adoption and how very much her mother loved and wanted her. I don't care what Vito says or does. He is no longer the powerful Mafia godfather but an ailing, frail old man who doesn't deserve to know his granddaughter. I will stay with Sophia Grace until she is better and then hope we can develop a loving relationship. I know You are in control of everything that happens, and we are not to question You, but I promise that if I'm given time to spend with my granddaughter, I will serve and worship You as I have always done."

CHAPTER 15

Grace spent the next nine months in the psychiatric ward at the Mayo Clinic. Every day, Anna Gambino sat by her granddaughter's side praying. Although Grace had no clue who the elderly woman was, she had grown attached to her and looked forward to seeing her.

"I don't know who the woman is that visits me every day, other than her name is Anna, but she is the sweetest woman in the world. Why would a perfect stranger come here every day?" Grace asked the doctor.

Dr. Williams knew exactly who Anna was and what had occurred twenty-eight years ago in Palermo. He told Anna they had to be very careful of how and when they revealed the situation to his patient.

"You must be gentle with Grace. As she begins to regain her memory, the psychiatrist will work with you on the way to explain what happened twenty-eight years ago and who you really are.

Remember, Grace has been through a very, very

traumatic experience. Anything negative could throw her back again into the darkness, and we certainly don't want that."

Each day that went by, Grace showed signs of regaining her memory and began talking about a dog named Max and a little girl named Gabby.

When Tianna returned to New York, Anna made sure she contacted her daily, keeping her up on everything that was happening. She suggested Tianna visit Grace again and bring Max and Gabby to see if it would help trigger Grace's memory more.

Two weeks later, Tianna flew to Arizona toting her daughter Gabby and Max. When the three of them walked into Grace's room, Anna was sitting by the bed watching her granddaughter sleep.

"Ssssshhhh! My *bella* is sleeping," Anna said.

The minute Max saw Grace lying there he started to bark and jumped on the bed. When he licked her face, Grace opened her eyes.

At first, she just stared at the dog, not sure of who he was. Then Gabby squealed, "Aunt Gwace! Yewell up!"

At that moment, a light bulb went off in Grace's head, and she screamed, "Max! My baby boy, I've missed you sooooooo much. And Gabriella! You have grown so much, Gabby!" Grace looked over at Tianna and opened her arms, inviting her friend in.

"Ti! Where have you been?"

***

Dr. Williams agreed that seeing Max and Gabby was exactly what Grace needed, for from that day on, her memory slowly returned.

The last thing Grace remembered was receiving the Academy Award and then getting the news that Mattia, the love of her life, had been involved in a fatal plane crash.

When she realized she would never see Mattia again, she mourned for weeks. Grace missed him so much but knew that this, too, was something she had no control over. It was obvious God wanted Mattia back home with Him, and one day, they would be reunited.

The hospital chaplain was a Christian female named Sierra, who made daily visits to Grace. Sierra said that God had a grand plan for everyone, and if someone or something got in the way, He would remove it from the equation. Sierra also said that perhaps Mattia was not the person meant for Grace. When she said that, Grace became enraged.

"What do you mean he's not the right one? He was my soulmate. I will never find anyone that I love more than Mattia."

The chaplain told Grace there's a difference between needing and wanting. "You may not need a new dress, but you want it. It's the same with people. Although you may not want them, they may be the person you need."

After the chaplain left, Grace sat there mortified. Mattia *was* her soulmate and almost her husband, and she didn't think she would ever love a man again. It was obvious that God's plan for her was to remain single and never have children of her own, but Grace never could have guessed what the heavenly Father had planned for "the girl with the butterfly tattoo."

***

After spending more than nine months at the Mayo Clinic and seeing the progress Grace had made, Dr. Williams said it was time for Grace to leave. Not knowing where to go or what to do, Grace told Tianna, "I don't know where to go or what God wants me to do. I've been praying about it but still have no answer."

Meanwhile, back in Sicily, Vito Gambino was deteriorating quickly, and Anna knew it was time to return to Palermo. She didn't want to leave her granddaughter as they had become close in their own special way.

"Doctor, it is time for me to fly back to Palermo. My husband is dying, and as his wife, it is my duty to be with him when he leaves the world. Do you think I can now tell my granddaughter who I really am?"

"I think she is strong enough to handle the truth now. Just watch how you tell her. I'm sure it is going to come as quite a shock, and the last thing we want is to see Grace regress."

***

The last day that Grace was at Mayo was a beautiful spring day. Anna took her granddaughter to the Healing Garden—the place Grace loved the most—saying she had something important to tell her.

The serenity garden offered a natural space that was designed to bring the benefits of the outdoors to its patients. It was a therapeutic space that added to the physical, psychological, emotional, and social elements of well-being and maximizing recovery.

Grace loved going to the Healing Garden. She would go there each day after therapy, and every time, she would see a butterfly. But they were always bright and colorful—not like the dark one that appeared the night of the awards.

To her surprise, she discovered that her new friend, Anna, also loved the flying creatures. "Butterflies symbolize personal transformation, change, hope, renewal, and courage. They are also associated with new beginnings and fresh starts. In many cultures, butterflies are believed to be spirit messengers carrying important messages for those who see them," Anna told Grace.

The matriarch of the Gambino family was scared of how Grace would react when she told her the truth—that she was her grandmother and the mother of her mother who had died giving birth to Grace.

Anna wasn't sure how to begin the conversation when a monarch butterfly flew and landed on Anna's shoulder. Surprised, Anna said, "Thank You, Jesus, for sending me this sign. The monarch butterfly is the king of butterflies who rules alone. They are the smartest, strongest, and toughest of all butterflies. A monarch can travel or migrate twenty-five hundred miles, and although they are usually found in North America, storms have blown them to other continents. Perhaps, my little friend, you came to us from Palermo?"

Grace sat there with her mouth ajar. Although a butterfly had landed on her many times in her life, she never saw one land on another person like this one did to Anna. This particular monarch was the most beautiful butterfly Grace had ever seen. The brilliantly colored creature's wings spanned four inches and were deep orange with black borders and white spots along the edges. There were two black spots in the center of its hind wings, so Anna knew that this particular monarch was a male.

Anna assumed that not only was this a "whisper from God," giving her the encouragement and strength to tell her granddaughter what had to be told, but also a sign that her husband Vito needed her now.

"Grace, what I'm about to tell you will change your life drastically, honey. Please know that I have waited almost twenty-nine years for this day, and with the grace and guidance of God, what you are about to hear is the truth."

Anna made the sign of the cross and began. "Almost

twenty-nine years ago, a woman named Regina—my only child—gave birth to a beautiful baby girl. That baby was you."

At first, Grace thought she had heard wrong, but after seeing the look on the woman's face, she was assured it was the truth.

"Your name is Sophia Grace Gambino. Your mother got pregnant to a man named J.C.—a soldier who worked for your grandfather, Vito—the don of the Sicilian Mafia.

J.T. was already married with children, so he could not marry your mother. Gina wanted you so badly, but it was a disgrace to the family, so Vito hid you in our groceria for four months until you were born. You made your debut into the world four weeks early, so the midwife and myself were the only ones there to welcome you. My poor Regina developed complications and died giving birth, but she lived long enough to see your precious face and kiss you. I wanted to keep you and raise you as my own, but your grandfather is a stubborn, proud tyrant who gave me no choice. But there wasn't a day that went by when I didn't pray for you and think about how you were and who adopted you. I tried to find out, but the orphanage wouldn't tell me.

When I saw your face on the cover of *Sports Illustrated* saying, 'The girl with the butterfly tattoo,' I almost fainted. You see, your mama had the exact tattoo and so does your papa, Vito. It is the Gambino brand."

Anna saw the color drain from Grace's face from

pink to pale as the girl began to shake. "Do you want me to continue, honey, or is this too much to hear at once, Sophia—I mean Grace?"

"No, please continue. I always thought the tattoo was a curse, but now I know it was a blessing. It is a part of my family, and I am proud that I have it. Every time a butterfly would appear out of nowhere, it would warn me of an upcoming event. It usually always ends in a tragedy, but today, having a monarch butterfly land on you was a wonderful thing. I always called these "signs" or "whispers from God," and now I *know* that is exactly what they are. I wondered my entire life why I was given away. I thought my mother didn't love me."

"Your mother loved you with her whole heart, as I do. And your grandfather does, too, but he is just too darn stubborn to admit it. That's another thing, honey. Your papa, Vito, is dying of cancer, and I have to return to Italy immediately to be with him when he passes, for that is my duty. No matter what horrible things he has done, I took my vows under God, 'Till death do us part,' and I must go home. I want to take you back with me to meet him before he dies. Please come with me."

When Grace called Tianna and told her all about the conversation she had with her long-lost "nana," her friend cried.

"That's wonderful, Gracie. I knew all about it but was told to keep it a secret until you got better. Anna is a wonderful, sweet woman, and I know how much she loves you. Don't worry about Max. He is doing fine. Maybe slowing down a bit, but he's quite happy here."

***

It had been one year since Mattia's plane had crashed, and until recently, Grace had no recollection of what had happened. She was unaware of Mattia's funeral and his final wishes.

Mattia's mother flew her son's body back to Italy and buried him in the family mausoleum. When his last will was read, it divulged that he left the land he owned in Togo, Africa, to Grace, for he knew that was where she always wanted to live. He also left Grace the Montana ranch and a trunk full of personal keepsakes. Being appointed Grace's power of attorney, Anna handled all the details until her granddaughter was well enough to make any decisions.

The week after Anna told Grace about her mother and grandfather and why she was given up for adoption, the two women flew to Palermo. Everyone at the Mayo Psychiatry Department was sad to say goodbye to their favorite patient but happy to see her well again.

When Anna explained everything to Grace, she could accept everything her grandmother said except one thing: how could her grandfather rule one of the most horrific vile organizations on earth? To have people murdered and to be the one who ordered Grace's father killed was something she didn't think she could ever forgive.

THE EVOLUTION OF GRACE

That night, after her bags were packed, Grace got down on her knees and prayed, "Heavenly Father, please show me how I can forgive all the horrible things that my grandfather has done. I know You preach how important it is to forgive others as we have been forgiven by the blood of Your Son Jesus Christ, and with the grace and mercy shown to us, we are to start new with God. Although the act of forgiving Papa does not come easy, it is my choice as a Christian to do so. Please help me. In Jesus' name, I pray."

CHAPTER 16

As Anna and Grace hurried to Gate 9 to board an Alitalia flight to Sicily, the boisterous crowd silenced.

"Oh, my goodness. Isn't that girl over there the actress Grace Antonelli?" one teenage boy asked his friend. "You know, the girl with the butterfly tattoo?"

"I don't know, but she sure is *hot*!"

Grace and Anna were seated in first class in the front of the plane, Row 1—seats 1 and 2. As the hostess seated them, she stuttered, "Are…are…aren't you Grace Antonelli?"

"Yeah, you're the girl with the butterfly tattoo. I would know that face anywhere," the male steward said.

Grace still couldn't believe she was on her way to Sicily—the place where she had been born. Sitting next to her was her grandmother, Anna Gambino—a woman she never knew existed until recently.

It was all happening so fast that Grace was having a hard time trying to decipher all that occurred the past year.

Having amnesia and being in a coma for so long not only robbed Grace one year of her life, but when she awoke, it was to a completely different world.

Her real name was Sophia Grace Gambino. She was born on July 4, 1954, to Regina Gambino—an eighteen-year-old single woman in Palermo, Sicily. Her mother died bringing her into the world, and then she was put up for adoption.

Gambino was her family name and the most renowned name in Sicily. Her grandfather, Vito Gambino, is the ex-head of the Sicilian Mafia. Her grandmother, Anna, is a loving, selfless, compassionate woman who should be anointed a saint for the life she endured by her tyrant husband.

As Grace watched her grandmother asleep, her heart melted. Her nana permeated peace, tranquility, and unconditional love. The lady was quite beautiful, and Grace knew that when she was young, she must have been the most beautiful girl in the village.

She wondered if her papa ever loved her nana or if he just wanted her to be his trophy. What did Anna's daughter—Grace's mother, Gina—look like, and what did Grace's father look like? If he was in the Mafia, he must have been ruthless and cold-hearted, for anyone who killed another person, sold illegal drugs, and promoted prostitution was not a godly man.

The Bible says that gangs who commit themselves to

one another in criminal activity such as drugs, prostitution, extortion, and theft are from the devil. This was nothing new for like-minded people have always tended to band together since the Tower of Babel (Genesis 11).

During the long flight to Sicily, Grace was unable to sleep. From time to time, her mind would wander and think about Mattia, and she would start to cry, but that is when the almighty Father would step in and take her by the hand.

Grace wasn't sure how to approach her grandfather. After all, he was the reason she was sent away. So how could she be kind to him?

But that's when a "whisper from God" said, "Remember that God forgave us, and after everything man did to Jesus, He turned the other cheek."

So if Jesus Christ could forgive man for what we did to Him, then certainly Grace could forgive Papa.

A limo was waiting at the Boccadifalco Airport in Palermo for the two women. The young Italian driver reminded Grace of Antone. Seeing the look on her granddaughter's face, Anna asked, "What's wrong, *bella*?"

"Nothing, Nana. I was just thinking about my other family in New York—you know, Tianna, Antone, Gabby, and Max; I miss them so much."

"Well, perhaps we can fly them all here for a visit soon. Let's wait and see what happens with Papa. And don't worry. The nurse said Vito hasn't said one word for the past month, so I don't think he will be loud or nasty. I think those days are gone. His mind is still there, but he hasn't talked. The doctor said he thought maybe Vito was mourning not having me there, but I told him Vito never cared before, so why should he now?"

***

As the limo drove up the long, winding driveway to the Gambino estate, Grace gasped. Yes, she had been to some of the most beautiful homes in the world, but this is where her mother was raised and lived. This was home to her mama, Gina, and her grandparents. It was the Gambino legacy, and Grace was now very much a part of it.

The sixteenth-century Italian Renaissance architecture gave way to numerous cupolas and tall, narrow windows topped with ornamented pediments. When the butler opened the door, he cried, *"Cristo Tariq, saperlo un po' in anticipo sarebbe stato carino. Sei tu, Regina!"*

"No, Antonio, this is not Regina. This is Regina's daughter, Sophia Grace, our granddaughter," said Anna.

Anna took Grace by the hand as the two women walked into the main bedroom where Vito Gambino lay dying.

Anna walked over to him and kissed both cheeks. "Ciao, Vito. I am back home now and have brought someone I want you to meet."

When Vito opened his eyes and saw Grace, tears began rolling down his face. "Regina! *Mia figlia!*" he said as he opened his arms.

Grace stood there for a minute before she walked over and hugged her grandfather. "Papa, it's me, your granddaughter," Grace sobbed. "Sophia Grace."

"My granddaughter? But she was sent to America long ago. Can this be?"

As Grace turned, Vito saw the tattoo and cried, "Dear God, it truly is my baby's baby. This is a miracle."

It was a touching, heartfelt moment as Vito, Anna, and Grace joined together in a group hug and cried. Anna was shocked at how receptive and loving Vito had been to Grace. She had prayed to God for years to soften her husband's hard heart, and once again, the Lord answered her prayers.

Vito's doctor said he had seen a miracle or two in his life, but this topped them all, for after meeting his granddaughter, Vito's health drastically improved. Of course, it didn't end the cancer, but for the next two years, Vito talked, laughed, loved, and even prayed with his wife and granddaughter. Miraculously, Vito was now a God-fearing man who prayed every day, asking God for forgiveness.

One day, Vito summoned a priest and friend, Father John, to his home.

"Father, I have done some horrific things in my life. Although I never held a gun or actually killed a person myself, it was me who gave the orders. How can God ever forgive me? I gave my only grandchild away, for I was ashamed of Gina getting pregnant to a married man, and

I've treated my wife horribly. And I cheated on Anna our entire marriage, but I always loved her. I am a horrible person who was ruled by Satan himself and not our heavenly Father."

For the first time in their marriage, Anna saw her husband cry.

Father John told Vito, "Vito, although it is true that you were a horrible human being—yes, Satan had his hands on you—our God allowed these things to happen. Why? Despite all the horrific things you have done, a person can find redemption in the eyes of the Lord. In Romans 5:8, Paul tells us that God demonstrates His love for us in this: 'While we were still sinners, Christ died for us.' This means that even those who commit heinous acts can receive God's mercy and grace if they turn to Him with repentance and faith."

"But how can this be, Father? The sixth commandment says not to kill, and although I may not have pulled the trigger myself, it was because of me that those people were killed."

"Vito, our God is a just God. His righteousness is an attribute that leads Him to do only those things that are right. One of the benefits of salvation is you get endued with the righteousness of God. He can forgive anyone who truly repents and puts his faith and trust in Christ for salvation."

"Father, I want to be baptized. Is that possible? A sinner

like myself can be born again?"

"Of course, Vito. I will be honored to baptize you."

Anna and Grace were ecstatic. As they sat by his bed, Father John took holy water from his case and poured it over Vito's head three times as he recited, "Vito Gambino, I baptize you in the name of the Father (pours water the first time) and of the Son (pours water a second time) and of the Holy Spirit (pours water over Vito's head a third time).

"Grace, we have just witnessed a true miracle from our heavenly Father."

Every afternoon, Grace would take her grandfather in his wheelchair to the botanical garden located on their property, where they would laugh, pray, and catch up on the years they were apart.

Grace's thirtieth birthday was approaching, and her grandparents wanted to give her a special gift. When they asked her if she wanted a car, jewelry, or a horse, Grace surprised them by saying, "Papa, all I want is a life-size replica of Jesus on the cross. We can have it carved out of one of the pine trees on our property where we can go and pray to Him every day. After all, He is the reason we are all here together as a family."

Vito hired Giovanni, the best woodcarver in the country, to design the life-size cross. He used Giovanni once before to make the wooden gates to the entrance, protecting intruders from entering the Gambino estate.

Giovanni cut and kiln-dried the logs and then stained

and coated the replica of Christ on the cross. From the bottom to the top, the replica stood approximately seven feet tall. Giovanni followed what was written in Luke 24:39 (Christ was nailed, not tied, to the cross by His wrists, not His hands like many thought).

To make the replica of the cross as close to the one Christ was nailed to, the carver used three different types of wood in honor of the Trinity. Based on the limited non-Christian sources he could find, the carver erected an upright stake where the hands of Christ were raised vertically and nailed above His head, a scaffold-type structure made of vertical planks, and an X-shaped cross that straddled the feet. When it was finished, it was spectacular.

Anna had the gardener plant a variety of Alyssum, Aster, Butterfly weed, Dinathus, Goldenrod, Lavender, Marigold, Queen Anne's lace, and Zinnia around the base of the cross for these were the plants that attracted Grace's favorite thing in the world—the butterfly.

The day that Sophia Grace Gambino, also known as Grace Antonelli, turned thirty years old, her grandparents took her down to see her present for the first time. When Grace saw the cross, she burst into tears and fell to her knees.

"Thank you, Papa and Nana. This is the best gift I ever got in my life. No, it is the second-best gift. Having my family here with me is the first!"

CHAPTER 17

For the next two years, life at the Gambino estate was as perfect as it could possibly be. Although Vito was still battling cancer after he was reunited with his granddaughter, he was a different man. He was no longer mean; instead, he was a gentle, kind soul who treated everyone, especially Grace and Anna, with love and respect. Anna couldn't believe that this was the same man and had to pinch herself to make sure this wasn't a dream.

People in their village got word about the drastic change in the man who was once the cruelest Mafia don and couldn't believe it.

"It is all because of you, Grace, that Papa is now a child of God," said Anna.

"No, Nana. It is not because of me. It is our Father in heaven who changed Papa, for with God, nothing is impossible," Grace said.

When Vito was diagnosed with cancer, he gave his resignation to the Cosa Nostra. Although it's almost impossible for a member of the Mafia to get out of the *famiglia*, Anna contacted the pope.

The induction into the Cosa Nostra is shrouded in quasi-religious symbolism with blood oaths intended to act as a "second baptism." But when Anna discovered her husband was dying of cancer, she met with the pope and begged him to visit Vito and give him his blessing.

"Murder is a grave sin, Anna, but it is not bigger than other sins. God forgives all sinners, including murderers, provided they come to Him in humility and ask for forgiveness and repentance," Pope Giuseppe told her.

When the pope got word that Vito Gambino, once the most ruthless Mafia don, had been baptized and was now a born-again Christian, he came to give Vito his blessing and asked the Lord to forgive him for all the bad he had done. Anna said, "You see, Grace, with God, the impossible is possible. Your grandfather, who once was a cruel murderer, is now a loving child of God. My life is now complete, and I am ready to go home when God calls me. The only thing missing is your mama, Gina. But we will see her again in heaven, honey."

"Oh no, Nana. You better not be going anywhere soon. We have so much more to do together. My life is here with you and Papa now."

****

It was a brisk November day when, once again, Grace

Antonelli's life would take another life-changing pivotal turn.

Grace went down to the garden and sat on the bench in front of the cross. That morning, Papa told her he was tired and wanted to rest and would not be going with her to do their daily prayers. Anna also said she was extraordinarily tired and climbed into Vito's bed to lie with him.

Seeing her grandparents together made her heart smile. As she began giving thanks to the Lord, two butterflies flew together and landed on her lap. At first, she was startled, for never before had two butterflies appeared together.

When they flew off side by side into the sky, Grace knew that something was terribly wrong. She ran back to the house and was met at the door by the housekeeper, Nina, hysterically crying. "Grace, come quickly. Vito and Anna lie cold in their bed. They are not moving. Oh, *mio Dio*."

When Grace entered her grandparents' bedroom, Dr. Marino, the family doctor, was shaking his head.

"I'm so sorry, Grace. Your papa and nana have gone home to be with their Maker. May God bless them."

Dr. Milano caught Grace as she fainted and began administering smelling salts.

As her grandparents were being taken out on a stretcher, Grace screamed, "Nana! Papa! Please wake up. You cannot take them from me, God. You have taken everyone I have loved in my life. Please take me, too, for I want to die too."

PART V:

THE BUTTERFLY SANCTUARY

CHAPTER 18

Grace expected the death of her grandfather, but when she walked into the bedroom and saw her nana lying alongside her husband, the traumatized woman let out a high-pitched shrill.

It looked like a scene out of a movie she had once watched where two elderly people lie dying next to each other. Vito's arm was wrapped around Anna, who was in a fetal position.

"Nana! Papa! Please don't leave me too."

Dr. Marino, the Gambino's personal physician, walked over and put his arm around Grace. "I'm so sorry, Ms. Gambino. This is totally unexpected. I expected Vito to pass, but there was no indication that Anna would leave this world so soon too. When she was diagnosed with cancer one and a half years ago, she refused treatment. I warned her that the cancer could spread at any time, but she said she had to fly to America, for that was more important. I had no idea about you, as did anybody else here, for your grandparents kept the secret hidden for decades. Nobody knew of a granddaughter until Anna brought you back here last year. I assumed she told you of her cancer, but knowing Anna, I see why she didn't. Your grandmother was one of the most unselfish, loving, God-fearing women I have ever met. After her daughter Regina—your mother—died, Anna was never the same. There wasn't one day she didn't go to Immaculate Conception Church here in town. She was the most religious woman I knew who believed that God was in control of everything. Yes, your papa was a cruel man. He was born into the horrid organization and had no choice but to take it over when his father was gunned down. I knew that deep down inside, Vito was a good man, but once you are sworn into the Mafia you are pretty much married to it. Father Giuseppe, the pastor at Immaculate, is a personal friend of mine, and he also loved your grandmother. How could you not? She was not only beautiful on the outside, but she was more beautiful on the inside. Father didn't like what Vito did and the way he treated your nana, but Anna stood by her husband until the very end. Love really is the greatest gift God has given man. The love your grandparents had was a love/hate relationship, but through all of his indiscretions, there was only one woman Vito loved, and that was Anna. I'm not sure what your plans are with the Gambino estate, but anything you need help with, please call me. I feel that is the least I can do for Anna. You see, I was in love with your grandmother. Ever since the first time I saw her in the village—before she met Vito—I was enamored with her. She knew how I felt about her, but when you are given to a man in a made marriage, you have to adhere to your parents' wishes. Anna loved me too. We were young and silly fifteen-year-old children, but I know the love we had for each other was not just puppy love. Of course, nothing ever became of it, for I was just a poor village boy and couldn't compete with your grandpa. He was the most handsome boy in the village and, of course, the most powerful. The very last time Anna and I were together will be etched in my mind and heart forever. We were sitting under our oak tree in the park—the place we would sneak away to once a week—talking and fantasizing about maybe getting married one day. It was the last day I would ever be with my Anna, for when her father was told we were together, Vito forbid her ever to see me again. You look like Anna did when she was younger. Yes, you have the Gambino beauty like both she and your mother, but with you, there is a special beauty that comes from within. That is rare! There's a letter over there on Anna's vanity table addressed to you, Grace."

Grace walked over and picked up the letter. Her hands were shaking so badly she couldn't open the letter, so Dr. Marino opened it and handed the letter to Grace. It had been dated one week earlier, and on the outside of the envelope, it read Sophia Grace.

> To our dear granddaughter, Sophia Grace,
>
> If you are reading this letter, papa and I have gone home to be with our heavenly Father

and our precious daughter, Regina. I know Papa was hanging on to life, for he wanted to see you again and apologize for everything he did to you and your mother years ago.

At that time, Vito was a heartless, ruthless ruler, and for the longest time, I couldn't stand to look at him, but ever since you came here, he has been a different man.

He prayed to our Father to forgive him for the horrible things he has done, and I'm sure the Lord has, for He is a forgiving God. I read the Bible to Vito every night since I returned. That was something he would never let me do before.

He especially liked when I would read Nehemiah 9:17—"But thou art a God ready to pardon, gracious and merciful, slow to anger, and of great kindness, and forsookest them not."

The tears began running down Grace's face like a broken faucet. She put down the letter to dry off the tears and then picked up the letter and resumed reading.

Your grandfather has done some horrific things in his life, but when he asked me for forgiveness, of course, I forgave him, for who am I to judge and not forgive? If the Lord could forgive him, I certainly could.

One of my favorite sayings is Philippians 3:13. "Brethren, I count not myself to have apprehended: but this one thing I do, forgetting those things which are behind, and reaching forth unto those things which are before."

You must try to forget all the bad that happened to you in the past and move forward. Do not mourn more than a day for us. We want you to look forward to all the wonderful things that lie ahead for you.

God created each one of us and gave us a purpose. Although you may not know what your true purpose may be just yet, have patience, for God will reveal it.

You were given a very special life—that is why you have the butterfly tattoo, for it symbolizes beauty, freedom, and gentleness, which you have.

So, my dear nipotina, please find it in your heart to forgive Papa and know how sorry he is. Although we are heartbroken to leave you, we anxiously wait to see our Regina again. And also we want you to know how very proud we are of you. You are not only beautiful on the outside, but you are just as beautiful on the inside.

It was me who sent money every month. I

wanted to make sure you were financially okay, so whatever you did with that money was yours to do. You will not need it, though, for everything Papa and I have goes to you. It is quite substantial. Even more than you could imagine.

The entire Gambino estate in Palermo is yours and all the money we have—which is well over fifty million dollars. Do whatever you want with it, but I hope you put it to some worthy cause.

I have lived a good life, never wanting for anything, but there was one thing missing—I wanted to be reunited with my daughter again and to find you and tell you the truth of what happened the day you were born.

I worried every single day about who had adopted you—if they were godly people who gave you a good life and brought you up to know the Lord.

When I saw your picture on the cover of Sports Illustrated, I hired a detective to find where you lived and your personal information so my lawyer could wire you money every month.

You are all that is left of the Gambino legacy. I was hoping that one day you would meet and fall in love with the man God picked especially for you and to have children who would carry on our name.

Perhaps the Lord didn't want that, for the Gambino name was soiled because of Papa's evil ways. I didn't approve of what Papa did, and for fifty years, I prayed he would leave the Mafia and have a simple life. But when you are in, it is almost impossible to get out. The only reason Papa was able to step down was because he was diagnosed with cancer. That was not the way I wanted him to leave the organization, but I found out long ago it doesn't matter what you want—if it is not what God wants, it will not happen.

I hope you follow your heart, Grace, and do what makes you happy.

Pray before you make any decisions and ask God for guidance, for He will never steer you wrong.

I wish we could have spent more years as a family together, but now that I have found you, I can die in peace.

Papa was constantly attacked and enticed by Satan; thus, he chose to do the horrible things he did. Satan is the king of liars who kills, steals, and destroys human beings. Always remember the three areas Satan uses bait to destroy a person's life—the lust of the flesh, the lust of the eyes, and the pride of life. Throughout your life, you will be tempted by the deceiver to sin.

Ultimately, Satan wants you to believe in three lies: You are powerless over circumstances, you are a victim to an unloving God, and God has abandoned you. The king of darkness will tempt a person where they are the weakest, and he is capable of appearing in all kinds of different forms. You must never forget that God loves you no matter what condition you are in, and He will always prevail over the devil.

Papa is quickly fading now. He waited for us to return to Palermo so that he could see you and say how very sorry he was. Yes, Papa found the Lord—thanks to you!

I didn't tell you, but over a year ago, I was also diagnosed with stage 4 metastatic breast cancer and refused treatment.

It is now time for me to go to my heavenly home and be with your mother, my daughter, Regina. One day, we will all be waiting by the pearly gates to welcome you home—then we will be a complete family, but until then, please take care of yourself.

God will most surely let you know what it is you are to do with your life. Although you have had all the fame and wealth anyone could dream of, I know there is something special you are to do. Always be proud of your Gambino birthmark and what it represents, and whenever a butterfly lands on you, know that it's me!

I'll love you forever,

Nana

CHAPTER 19

After the death of her grandparents, Grace was confused, numb, and frightened. She was thirty-one years old and all alone in the place she had been born—Palermo, Sicily. Seven thousand miles from New York City and from the only few people she had left in the world, Grace Gambino once again had come to a crossroads in her life.

Uncertain about her future and what path she should take, Grace knew that a massive, pivotal decision would have to be made, but until then, there were so many things she needed to handle.

Grace retained all of her grandparents' employees, for they had been working decades for the Gambinos, and this was the only home they had known.

Every night, Grace would go and sit in the Bobolia Gardens. The terraced garden covered twenty-five acres behind the Gambino estate. This was also Nana and Papa's favorite place to go and pray.

The Bobolia combined landscape gardens and carefully

manicured "nature" with the formal parterre, architectural follies, and water features common to Renaissance gardens. It was all tied together by promenades and more intimate paths that make strolling these gardens a welcome respite from the city.

From the top of the gardens, you could see the entire city of Palermo.

A massive amount of tall cypresses flanked by chestnut, cork oaks, and pines led down the oval piazza, and indigenous plants to northern Italy were planted and could be seen under a large statue of Mary holding baby Jesus.

About half a mile from the entrance were winding walks designed for strolling and worship. At the end of the longest walk was a maze enclosed by shrubbery and trees where the wildlife called home.

Every night, Grace would go to the gardens and pray to God for guidance and wait on His word of what it was Grace was to do. It was exactly nine months after her grandparents' death when she finally got the answer. It was a chilly evening, and the sky was filled with sparkling stars. As Grace was praying, a butterfly flew down from the sky and landed on the bench where she was sitting.

It was a large blue morpho butterfly. As the creature sat on the bench, flapping its wings, it didn't go anywhere, so Grace reached down and gently picked it up. This particular creature's wings were bright blue with lacy black edges.

Ever since butterflies started appearing to Grace, she

began to study the insects to learn more about them. She knew that a blue morpho—like the one here—originated in the forests of Central and South America, so it was far away from its home. How did it get here, and why was it in Palermo?

Grace sat there for what seemed like hours as the butterfly fluttered its wings but did not fly away. Finally, the majestic creature flew onto Grace's shoulder. As its front wings fluttered, it began producing a crackling sound. Grace sat perfectly still, not wanting to make any sudden move that might scare the aphid away.

"What is it, my friend? What are you trying to tell me?" she asked.

She made eye contact as the butterfly flew away, high into the sky, before disappearing in the clouds.

She had read that butterflies had two different types of eyes—one that focuses on objects and another one used as their main eyesight. Their eyesight was very crucial to their survival; while humans perceive between forty-five and fifty-three flickers per second, aphids' rate is 250 times greater, giving them an excellent, continually updated image.

A butterfly's wings are covered by thousands of tiny scales, and these scales reflect light in different colors, but under its wings is a layer of chitin—the same protein that makes up an insect's exoskeleton.

The sad thing Grace discovered was that a butterfly has

only two or four short weeks to live. However, monarchs can live as long as nine months.

"Why does such a harmless, beautiful creature live only a short time?" Grace often asked herself.

When she discovered the reason, it changed Grace Gambino Antonelli's way of thinking. Unlike humans, the main purpose of a butterfly is to make babies so the species can continue. This is an urge that God built in them to let them know what to do and how and when.

A butterfly ages quickly. As it emerges and goes out to feed, mate with other butterflies, and lay its eggs, their purpose in life has been completed.

It has achieved what it needed to do, and it dies soon after. Very sad indeed, but at least they served their God purpose, and man can enjoy them while they are alive.

That night, when Grace knelt to say her prayers, she asked God for guidance on what to do. As she got up, a bright flash flashed in the room. Although she did not hear the answer through words, Grace knew that God had spoken to her.

She was to build a butterfly sanctuary on the Gambino estate where people from all over the world could come. Besides being a place where butterflies of all species could dwell, the sanctuary would be a sacred space for helping others help themselves to transform where they are in their lives.

The butterfly sanctuary would be a place where

thousands of free-flying butterflies could flutter, fly, emerge, and grow. It would be a climate-controlled conservatory where man could escape to and stroll through an enclosure, educating and encouraging people to support the wondrous creation and preservation of natural butterfly habitats.

She would call it "Anna's Butterfly Sanctuary" in honor of her family and her nana's love for the creature. After all, when God created Grace, He etched a butterfly into her skin as he did to her Papa and Mama. Perhaps this was the reason.

After meeting with dozens of contractors, Grace hired Guido Mascara, the best in the country, to build the butterfly sanctuary. The facility would be constructed over five acres behind the Gambino estate. There would be an open and outdoor enclosure for the many different species of butterflies that could flutter free amongst the hundreds of pollinated flowers, and a winter habitat would be constructed too. It would be an environment where butterflies could safely lay their eggs and pollinate and where caterpillars can also grow, eat, and eventually retreat into their chrysalises.

Nectar-rich flowers would be planted, along with alyssum, pentas, salvia and zinnia—a butterfly's favorite flowers. Outside the main building, two distinct gardens were designed to resemble the significant gardens of Japan, and a small island with a pond surrounded by carefully positioned stones would be home to koi fish and seven living species of swans: the trumpeter swan, tundra swan,

Bewick's swan, whooper swan, black swan, black-necked swan, and mute swan.

When Guido began laying out his plans, Grace hired Maria Castalano, the top lepidopterist in Sicily, to help her with the plans from beginning to end. Ms. Castalano specialized in the order of Lepidoptera, which is comprised of 160,000 species of butterflies and moths. The Lepidoptera are the most widely studied order of invertebrates and have been for more than four hundred years.

"Why are you so interested in butterflies, Miss Gambino?" Castalano asked Grace.

"I have always had a special connection with butterflies," Grace answered but left it at that. She was afraid of what Maria would think if she told her how a butterfly appeared periodically to warn and alert her of danger.

"My nana also loved butterflies, and she passed away recently, so I was inspired to build this sanctuary in her honor. And I would love to educate other people about this wonderful creature."

By the end of the following year, Anna's Butterfly Sanctuary was up and running.

When the sanctuary was completed, Anna threw a grand opening promoted by wide media broadcast. It was advertised in *Vogue Italia, Panorama, IO Donna, Thy Magazine*, and *L'Illustrazione Italiana*.

Grace booked the band Gipsy Kings to appear on opening day, along with a variety of clowns to entertain the children, and Maria Castalano would provide seminars and workshops to educate patrons on the butterfly. A twenty-five-foot sign was erected that read Anna's Butterfly Sanctuary, with a photo of Anna Gambino.

The opening was a huge success, amassing a hundred thousand dollars that Grace donated to The Immaculate Conception Church in Palermo.

Ever since the death of her grandparents, Anna began attending morning mass at The Immaculate Conception and receiving communion. She felt total peace when she was in church and soon became friends with the priest, Father Dominic Scolierri. Not needing the money the sanctuary brought in, Anna was going to donate 100 percent of the earnings to the church.

"Grace, you are such a blessing to our town. Ever since you moved here, you have touched many people's hearts. You are truly a gift from our Lord. What you did with the butterfly sanctuary and donating the money to my church is something sent from above, and I will never be able to thank you enough. You are truly a child of God and an angel on earth."

Grace's face turned a pretty shade of crimson. "Thank you, Father, but I'm thankful I could honor my nana in this way. I know Papa had done some very, very bad things in his life, but in the end, he asked the Lord for forgiveness and to come into his heart, and he was saved."

"You are the reason for that, my dear. Yes, Vito did

many horrific things, and the town did not forget about them. In the beginning, they were against anything that had the Gambino name on it, but your grandmother and you are loved by everyone. What is on your calendar, dear, now that the butterfly sanctuary is up and running? I hope you will remain here in Palermo."

"Father, I will be taking a trip to the States to see my best friend and dog for a few weeks, and then I'm not sure what I'm going to do. I am not continuing my acting career, for without my Mattia, I have no desire."

"You were blessed with a fairy-tale life, Grace. You were a model and a famous actress and are now the lone heir to the Gambino empire. Why do you not look happy?" Father Dominic asked.

"Father, although the good Lord has provided me with everything material a person could possibly want, there has always been something missing in my heart. I never loved anyone like I loved Mattia, and I'm not ashamed to say I never slept with a man."

The look that came over the priest's face was priceless.

"That is nothing to be ashamed of, Grace. In fact, it is a rarity for a woman to save herself for the right man today. I'm sorry you and Mattia never got the chance to marry, but it is obvious that God has other plans for you. Our Lord even knows the number of hairs you have in your head. You see, when you were born, your life was mapped out. In Jeremiah 29:11 it says, "For I know the thoughts that I think toward you, saith the Lord, thoughts of peace, and not of evil, to give you an expected end."

It's obvious that God is saving you for something much bigger in life. Whenever you get anxious, get down on your knees and say Psalm 46:10."

"I know, Father. That is my favorite psalm—"Be still, and know that I am God."

CHAPTER 20

When Grace got off the plane at JFK Airport, Tianna was waiting for her with Gabby and Max. When the girl and dog saw Grace walk up to the car, they both shrilled with delight.

"Oh my! What a wonderful welcome! I've missed the both of you soooooo much!" Grace said as she picked up Max.

"Well, what about me? Am I chopped liver?" Tianna laughed as she put Grace's Louis Vuitton suitcase in the trunk.

"You *know* I'm thrilled to see my 'sister by another mister.'" Grace chuckled.

"Well, come on… tell me what the heck you've been up to besides opening Sicily's number one tourist attraction. Anna's Butterfly Sanctuary is all the world news talks about. I'm so proud of you, Grace, and I *know* your grandmother would have been too."

"It is really something to see, Ti. I mean, when you

walk through the door, you are greeted by thousands of different types of butterflies that represent new beginnings. The feeling of total peace you feel at Anna's Butterfly Sanctuary is magical. I always questioned why I was born with a butterfly tattoo, and at one time, I was ashamed of anyone seeing it. I hated it and thought it was not from God but from the devil himself."

"Yeah, I remember the first time I saw it when we were doing the Guess ad. I thought it was eerie-looking and made fun of it. I'm so sorry, Grace."

"Love is never having to say you're sorry, Ti. Anyway, it brought us together, and you are and will forever be my best friend—in this life and in the next.

Whenever a butterfly would appear, it was a warning that something was about to happen. Most of the time, it was not a good thing, but at other times, it introduced me to a new beginning. Like my mother would always say, 'When one door closes, another opens,' and they certainly did!

A butterfly represents a transformation as it evolves from a wooly caterpillar to a colorful butterfly. Their metamorphosis is a metaphor for rebirth, but depending on whom you ask, their spiritual symbolism runs deeper than that.

These majestic creatures show us how we can go within ourselves to dissolve old forms and morph while rebuilding and evolving ourselves. Just like man—caterpillars have no way of knowing what's coming their way next.

Butterflies represent freedom, allowing death and rebirth to take place, and it's amazing how the different cultures fixate on them and their spiritual meaning. In fact, the Aztecs offered incense to an image of the sun with a butterfly in a golden circle. In Christianity, there's a link between the transformation of a butterfly and the death and rebirth of Jesus Christ, and in the African culture, a butterfly's metamorphosis is often thought of as a symbol for transformation."

"Wow! Thanks for the nature lesson. So, Madam Butterfly, what exactly is your aphid telling you to do now?" Tianna laughed.

***

For the next few weeks, Grace thought long and hard about what Tianna had said. What were the butterflies trying to tell her? What new adventure was awaiting and where was God going to take her next?

Grace was now in her thirties, and as she discovered, time doesn't slow down for anyone. The only man she had ever romantically loved was gone; the only parents she ever knew were dead, and now her birth grandparents had been called back home.

Granted, Grace Gambino had done a lot in her thirty years on earth, but what was she to do with the rest of her life? She founded the butterfly sanctuary in honor of her family, and surprisingly, it was very successful. It didn't need Grace to be there, for she had hired Maria to run it, and she was doing a fantastic job.

The Gambino house would remain vacant, so anytime Grace wanted to visit, the house was waiting. She kept her grandparents' employees on the payroll—a house cleaner, a butler, and a gardener—for they had been loyal, dedicated employees also mourning the death of her grandparents. She knew God created everyone with his own special purpose, so what was hers?

Grace missed attending morning mass in Palermo and especially her talks with Father Dominic. Other than her father and Mattia, Father Dominic was the only man Grace felt comfortable talking with.

They would talk about God the Father and His Son, Jesus Christ, most of the time. Grace would get so sad when they discussed how Jesus was betrayed by one of His own and the horrific and painful death He endured.

One day, Grace asked Father, "Father, why did God allow all these things to happen to His Son? He could have stopped it, but He didn't. A parent is supposed to protect their child, but God allowed the mocking, scourging, and Jesus being nailed to the cross. I can't even bear to think about what poor Christ went through," she sobbed.

"My child, when our first parents, Adam and Eve, committed sin, they were condemned to die, for in God's government, 'the wages of sin is death.' God is love, and

His mercy is great, but He is also just, and in order to uphold His attribute of holiness, He must judge and punish sin. But instead of the sinner dying, according to God's law, Jesus offered himself to die on His behalf."

When Grace stopped crying, Father continued, "Take time to reflect on Jesus Christ and His death for you, then by faith invite Him to come into your life."

"Father Dominic, I owe so much to Jesus, but I don't know how to thank Him for all the suffering He endured for me—a sinner?

"The greatest thing a Christian can do is to go out and make disciples for Christ. A disciple maker lives with the purpose and answers the call Jesus issued through the Great Commission, a charge given two thousand years ago to His disciples," the priest said.

And it was that very minute when Grace Gambino Antonelli finally discovered what her life's calling was.

***

"I think I know what my mission in life is, Ti. God whispered in my ear and told me He wants me to be one of His ambassadors—a disciple who goes out in the world to preach His message, imploring men and women everywhere to be reconciled to God."

"*Wow*! That is some heavy stuff, Grace. I mean, it sounds wonderful but it is completely different than how your life has been and how it is now. I mean, you have had all the luxuries and blessings in the world. Why would you want to give it up and live a simple, maybe even common life?"

"That's it. Don't you see, Ti? I *have* had all the glitz and glamour, but was I ever really happy? No, not really. I mean, I am grateful for everything, but all I ever wanted in the world was love.

I mean a *true* love that one can only get from Jesus Christ. The kind of love that Jesus had for His people. Not a feeling, a passion, lust, or a sentiment, but rather an action. I was happy when I was with Mattia and thought we would be together forever, but the Lord needed and wanted him more. You see, God will bring people into your life for a reason. He will bring someone in for a purpose, and once that purpose is accomplished, He may take them away. All I ever wanted was the kind of love that brought Jesus to the cross on our behalf. That is the only type of unconditional pure love one can have. I had to learn how to forgive those who abandoned me, for a true disciple forgives and knows that the Atonement of the Savior covers all sins and mistakes of each one of us."

"But where are you going to evangelize? In Palermo?"

"I'm not sure, but I will be having a come-to-Jesus talk with the Lord tonight," Grace said.

***

That night, while Grace was praying, something inexplicable happened. The room went dark except for a stream of light seeping through a crack in the window. Grace knew that whatever was happening was from God.

"Father in Heaven, please tell me what You want me to do with my life. I know that life is a journey, and we are only visiting here. Everything we have is not really ours but Yours. I feel so blessed to have lived the life I have, but there was always something missing. I thought it was the love of a man, but I realize now that *You* are the only man that will ever love me unconditionally."

Just then, a brilliant light encompassed the entire room, bringing a sense of total peace and love to Grace. She knew this was a sign from her Father. Once again, He was talking to her, and she now had the insight of her future. The next morning, Grace called the airlines and booked a one-way ticket to Togo, Africa.

CHAPTER 21
Togo, Africa
1986

"Are you sure you want to live on the other side of the world, Grace? Africa is so far away. What will you do there? Where will you stay? Will you be okay by yourself?" Tianna asked.

"Yes, yes, and yes," Grace answered. "I'm not sure what I'll do, but I know that whatever it is, it will be what I was born to do. You see, Ti, I can't explain it, but God whispered in my ear last night, and when I woke this morning, I had a strong conviction that whatever I am to do, Africa is the place I need to be. You know, if you listen, God will always answer you. He has never let me down, and I know He won't now. The butterfly sanctuary is doing great, and I am selling the Montana ranch, so I've tied all loose ends in my life. Besides you, Antone, Gabby, and Max, there is no one here for me. We can FaceTime weekly, and as far as Max goes, I could never take him away from Gabby. You all can come and visit me often as soon as I settle in. Gabby will be starting school soon, and I can leave knowing how happy you all are living on the ranch."

"Thanks to you, Grace, we are as happy as can be. We absolutely love our place, and we will forever be grateful. I have never ever met a person in my life as generous, loving, and compassionate as you are. I've said this before, and I'll say it again, when God created you, He added extra sugar, spice, and everything nice—and then, He threw away the mold because there is *no one* like you!"

Saying "so long" to her friends and dog was one of the hardest things Grace Antonelli ever did in her life. She made it a point to never say "goodbye," but instead say "so long," for she didn't want it to sound so final.

Grace learned the hard way that you never know when your last minute on earth will be. Every day of our life is numbered. God has numbered our days from before we were born until the day He calls us home.

As a believer, Grace knew that we are called to seek God's guidance and care in all things, knowing that He has already written the days of our lives in the book of life.

Seeing the sad look on Gabby's face was hard enough, but when Max saw Grace's suitcase, he knew she was leaving him again.

He must have sensed this time would be different because the fifteen-pound dog jumped onto Grace's lap and whimpered without ceasing.

"Gabby, don't look so sad. You can come visit Aunt Grace soon and play with all the animals. There's lions and tigers and bears—Oh *my*!"

"And *giwaffes*?" Gabby asked.

Laughing hysterically, Grace answered, "Yes, giraffes and horses and even elephants."

Gabby jumped up and down as Max ran in circles.

***

The next week, Grace left New York and flew first class from JFK Airport to Lome, the capital of Togo. She dressed down so that she wouldn't be recognized, wearing a blonde wig and an oversized pair of Ray-Ban sunglasses that covered most of her famous face.

She dressed in a loose jogging suit so that her voluptuous curves were hidden and, as usual, wore no makeup other than the red lipstick her mother told her never to leave the house without. Now, thinking about this crazy request, she laughed and wondered if it was an old-fashioned Italian thing.

Grace was thrilled when not one person at the airport noticed who she was, although everyone couldn't help but stare at her beauty, for, even covered up, her inner beauty and aura permeated through.

During the eighteen-hour non-stop flight, she never

slept a wink, for she had picked up a book at the airport and was totally enthralled by it. It was a Christian book called *Start Living Your Life Yesterday.*

When she read, "Don't be afraid that your life will end soon—be afraid that it will never begin. There is no greater gift that you can give or receive than to honor your calling. It's the reason you were born," it was the "aha" moment in her life she had been waiting for.

She was now thirty-two years old, and for such a young woman, she had seen it all, done it all, and experienced everything a person could possibly want. Yes, she was most likely going to be single for the rest of her life, but that is obviously what the Lord wanted.

One of her favorite quotes was from an unknown author—"It's better to have loved and lost than never to have loved at all," and Grace felt blessed to have experienced that true love in her lifetime with Mattia Russo.

After she deplaned and got her one piece of luggage, Grace hailed a taxi. The taxi driver was no older than twenty years old, and on the dashboard was the name Kofi.

"Where to, ma'am?"

Grace read the address from the piece of paper she had been carrying with her ever since Mattia died. In his will, he left Grace fifty acres of undeveloped land in Togo— "The address says 'Kara-off N16.' But that's all it says," she told Kofi.

He was silent for a minute before talking in a French

accent, "But, ma'am, there is nothing there but vacant land."

Being a multilingual country, most natives spoke French, but the other languages were Ewe and Kabiye.

As they drove through the Atakora Mountains, the long coastline consisted of sandy beaches and thickly planted coconut trees that were partially separate from the mainland. Grace discovered that Africa is a small continent, but what it lacks in size is made up of sheer beauty and cultural richness.

As they drove through the villages of Bassar, Narbale, and Niamtougou, Grace was shocked at the amount of poverty and undernourishment of the people. Children under the age of five were growth stunted, causing long-term negative impacts on their health and development.

The poverty level was the main cause of hunger, for the people could not afford food of sufficient quality or quantity. Now Grace understood why Mattia had flown to Africa twice a year to hunt animals to feed the children. Just thinking about Mattia made her sad. She didn't realize she was crying when Kofi asked, "Ma'am, are you okay?"

The children roaming the streets were filthy and half-clothed. Many had open sores and enormous distended bellies. Crying harder, Grace asked Kofi, "What is wrong here? Why are these children in such bad condition? This isn't the 1800s; it's 1984!"

"Ma'am, here in Africa, there are nearly one billion

people suffering from starvation, and we are in desperate need of building water wells. The water here is contaminated and causes waterborne diseases such as cholera and severe diarrhea. My little sister died last month from drinking the water. She got cholera and suffered a horrible death. And my baby brother is so malnourished you can count every bone in his body. His belly is distended because of kwashiorkor. His feet swell, his teeth are falling out, and there's a loss of pigmentation in his skin."

"Oh, dear God. How can this be happening today? What would it take to have wells built?" Grace cried.

Surprised that this young man knew so much, Grace asked him, "Kofi, how do you know so much? Are you in school studying about it?"

"Yes, ma'am, I am attending school to hopefully become a doctor one day, for I want to help our people here. And there are so many babies who have lost his or her mother and are orphaned with no place to go and no one to care for them," Kofi said.

After sitting a minute in silence, Grace asked, "How would you like to work for me, Kofi? I will buy you a car, and you will be my own personal driver. I will pay you well. How does a thousand dollars a month sound?" Grace asked him.

Kofi took out his calculator and figured out that the amount was 0.0016697361 in West African francs, as much as Kofi had earned in two years.

"I will need you to introduce me to people who can help me start building water wells. I have the money and will pay them well," Grace said.

***

When the taxi arrived at the address Grace had given Kofi, she knew why Mattia had bought the property. Although there was nothing on it, the fifty acres of land was something you would see on a postcard.

Togo itself stretches 370 miles from north to south, so owning 50 acres consumed a big part of it. On the land were large trees, including baobabs, mangroves, and reed swamps, and deer, monkeys, lizards, and birds enjoyed the sunny day.

Grace had booked a room at the Hotel de la Paix in Togo. She had Tianna look into the best hotels in Togo, for it was going to be Grace's temporary home for who knows how long.

Tianna contacted one of New York's best international traveling agencies, for she wanted to make sure Grace would be staying at the finest Togo offered. But in Togo, the best might be what the worst is in the States.

The agent said that in the 1970s, there was a government campaign to boost tourism, and Hotel de la Paix was one of the hotels competing on the coast.

When the taxi pulled in front of the hotel, a young man walked over and opened Grace's door.

"Welcome to the Hotel de la Paix, Miss Grace. We have been expecting you."

***

The hotel had a phone system based on a network of microwave radio relay routes supplemented by open-wire lines and cellular system. Grace called Tianna in New York. *"Ti. How are you, honey?"*

The last time Grace called Tianna, she discovered her dog Max had crossed the rainbow bridge. She mourned for days but remembered reading Isaiah 11:6–8 and Romans 8:18–25, which speak about the presence of animals in the life to come. God's promises portray a world to come in which animals will know the peace they, too, have longed for.

Grace got comfort in knowing that one day she would be reunited with her dog, but until that day, he was running in the clouds surrounded by her grandparents and parents.

"Well, it's about time! I was starting to think that maybe you were held captive by one of the tribesmen," Tianna laughed.

"How have you been? And how is Antone and my godchild, Gabby?"

"We are all fine. Gabby had a hard time losing Max, but we told her we would get her another dog someday. She is starting school next year, so she is looking forward to that."

"How is Antone doing?"

"He is fine, Grace, but he misses you too. Since he doesn't have to worry about a mortgage, he isn't killing himself working overtime. We can never repay you for buying us the ranch."

"I am just so happy that you are all happy. I'll come visit soon, but there is something I have to do first."

"Oh no! What is the girl with the butterfly tattoo up to now?" Tianna laughed.

CHAPTER 22

When Grace discovered how many people in Africa were dying due to the contaminated water they drank, washed clothes, bathed in and cooked, she was appalled.

Any water sources were more than an hour's walk from the village, and the contaminated water used by many people in Africa caused waterborne diseases such as cholera.

For women and girls, the lack of water meant laborious, time-consuming water collection, which risks their safety and takes away from time for education, family, or paying work.

Grace realized there could be no hope for a better future without clean, fresh water, so for the next five years, Grace Gambino took part in developing the largest water well project in Africa and named it The Gambino Wells of Hope.

Focusing on the rural hard-to-reach villages in Africa, Grace was hands-on in establishing efficient water sources. She learned that the technology used involved a simple pump system in order to teach the villagers how to maintain and repair the equipment.

The wells were built to last twenty to thirty years, so the villager residents were included in the well development process.

The week-long training was essential for the water well to continue functioning, and without hygienic practices, clean water doesn't stay clean. Without good sanitation habits, the water is easily tainted and loses its effectiveness in reducing health problems because people are still exposing themselves to disease.

A large drilling rig, truck, and professional crew were needed to actually dig the hole and then, because the water was so deep, a motorized pump was installed. Because the water is simply too heavy to lift from that depth with a hand pump, diesel generators, large electric pumps, piping, storage tanks, and housing could drive the total cost up to thirty thousand dollars or more.

The team that Grace hired installed a mechanical submersible water pump powered by solar panels, allowing for the distribution of water across many villages at one time without the need for local electricity or a traditional hand pump. After a well was installed, the drill team explained how the pump worked, how to keep the area clean, and who to call if it broke.

Each well was said to serve a minimum of five hundred people. That means it costs sixteen dollars to give a person clean water and help them live a long and healthy life. Of course, Grace paid for the entire project, which cost her around one million dollars. She used some of the money she had saved that her nana sent over the years, for she knew it would make her happy.

She felt blessed to have the means to help change people's lives for the better, and to her, that amount of money made a dramatic difference in so many lives.

Before The Gambino Wells of Hope was founded, the only wells in Africa were hand-dug. It was extremely laborious and time-consuming, for the people had to dig down more than fifty feet deep.

These wells were extremely dangerous to build and cost many lives of unskilled laborers. Also, they were often left uncovered and easily contaminated.

Besides providing much-needed fresh drinking water, building wells became focal points in the community, giving women a place to meet up and be able to interact.

***

King Ayu, the current Fiogan (king) of Togo, had been the ruler for over twenty years. In Africa, the king still reigned majestically due to their connection with tradition and as custodian of the history and culture of the people. Out of the fifty-four countries in Africa, Togo was one of three monarchies to maintain monarchial significance and remain as head of the government.

THE EVOLUTION OF GRACE

When King Ayu was told what Grace was doing, he sent for her. She was picked up in a car the king sent, and although it was considered the "nicest" vehicle he had, it rattled so loudly that Grace thought it surely would break down.

Grace arrived at King Ayu's compound in the middle of the afternoon, the hottest time of the day. In the streets, children of all ages were playing in the scorching heat with no water to drink.

When she got out of the vehicle, the children ran over, wanting to touch her. At first, she was apprehensive, for not only were they filthy, but most of them were covered with open seeping sores.

Grace knew that cholera was a grave problem in Togo, and the infectious and fatal bacterial disease can be fatal within hours once contracted. It was a horrible disease that usually was contracted by drinking the dirty water. Once infected, the person may have symptoms of diarrhea, dehydration, irritability, sunken eyes, a dry mouth, extreme thirst, little or no urinating, low blood pressure, dry skin, and an irregular heartbeat.

As she was the children malnourished and half-dressed with their bellies distended, Grace's heart and spirit broke.

One small girl about six years old ran over to Grace and hugged her leg. Her hair was matted and filthy, and she weighed no more than thirty pounds.

"Hello. What is your name?"

"Aamina."

"What a beautiful name. What does it mean?" Grace asked.

The girl's mother was standing nearby, holding a tiny boy who appeared to be around six months old. "The name means 'to feel safe,'" her mother said as the baby began to cry.

"Why is he crying? Is there something I can do?"

"Thank you, but he is hungry and thirsty. I'm afraid to give him any water. This is Langa, my son. He is two years old."

Grace was shocked, for the boy didn't look older than six months. She noticed something was wrong with Langa's eyes and asked his mother, "What is wrong with his eyes?"

"Lanka is blind. Several months ago, he drank from the ravine and went blind," she cried.

"Oh, Lord. I'm so sorry."

"Thank you, lovely woman, but almost our entire village is blind now because of the water."

Grace stood there as tears ran down her face. She picked up Aamina and hugged her, then reached into her pocket and handed her a piece of chocolate and then handed her brother a piece.

You would have thought Grace gave the girl filet mignon, for she gobbled it down in seconds and put her hand out for more, saying, "*Kutaka.*"

THE EVOLUTION OF GRACE

One of the first words Grace learned in Swahili was *kutaka*, which means "more." "I'm sorry, honey. I don't have anymore, but I promise to bring you more," Grace said as she kissed Aamina's head.

When Grace walked into the king's home, she wasn't sure what to expect. This was his castle, but the walls were soiled and filthy and looked like they hadn't been painted in years. The small rooms contained very little furniture and had an odor of musty mildew.

King Ayu was a pleasant-looking man who appeared to be around fifty years old. His wife, a former Miss Jamaica, was much younger and quite beautiful.

As they were sitting at the table eating dinner, there was a knock on the door. A man entered and begged the king for forgiveness for his nine-year-old son.

"What is the reason you are here?" King Ayu asked the man.

"My son threw a rock and broke a window. He didn't mean to. We are sorry, King. Please have compassion."

Although this was not anything severe, to Grace's surprise King Ayu directed one of his men to take the boy out back and give him ten lashes.

"What? You can't do that, King. This is not how you handle the situation," Grace said.

The entire room was silent, and the look on the king's wife's face said it all.

After a few minutes, King Ayu said, "Excuse me, but I am the king, and this is how we handle children who are undisciplined."

As Grace heard the boy's screams coming from the back, she excused herself to the bathroom. She cried and prayed to the Lord to end this cruel punishment.

When she returned to the dining room, the king said, "I have to give you credit, Miss Grace. Nobody questions or talks to me that way. Not only are you beautiful and smart, but you are very brave."

"What you are doing for my village is very commendable, and I am forever grateful. If there is anything I can do for you, please ask."

"Thank you, King Ayu. Yes, there is something. Please end this unnecessary, cruel discipline."

And from that day on, King Ayu was Grace Gambino's new best friend.

**

The next day, King Ayu sent for Grace, saying there was something very important she had to see. When she arrived, everyone from the village was waiting for the king. The women were dressed in their "Sunday's best." Although they looked like secondhand clothes from the Salvation Army, the women were proud to have them.

Grace was shocked to see how happy the village people

were. They had no money, little food, and no fresh water, and their wardrobe was limited to one or two pieces of dirty soiled clothing.

Some lived in man-made huts, while for others, the streets were their homes. Grace noticed they never complained or felt sorry for themselves—instead, they thanked God for everything they had. What a difference the Togolese were from the people she knew back home.

Having lived a life where it was all about what you wore, what kind of car you drove, and how big your house was—especially for the superrich, who never seemed to have enough and always wanted more—Grace had met many billionaires, and most of them were not happy. The fancy new Lamborghini, a wardrobe of designer clothes or an eight-carat diamond brought a smile to their faces, but once the "newness" wore off, they wanted more.

Why couldn't people be happy with what they had and quit trying to keep up with the Joneses? After all—have you ever seen a U-Haul pulling a hearse full of money or material things with them? No, you can't take it with you, and when God calls you home, you will leave the world exactly as you came into it. Like it says in 1 Timothy 6:7, "For we brought nothing into this world, and it is certain we can carry nothing out."

CHAPTER 23

When King Ayu arrived at the village, the people got down on their knees and worshipped him. The men played drums as the women and children danced with joy.

That particular day, a special celebration was to take place as a life-size statue of the king was being erected. It really was a wonderful piece of art, for it looked exactly like King Ayu—even down to his potbelly.

Off to the side was a large wooden table displaying a smorgasbord of food that the women had cooked and brought. There was Achu (a palm oil soup served with cow skin, oxtail, tripe, and eggplant), Akara (a food derived from peeled beans made into balls and deep-fried), Alloco (a fried plantain snack), and Asida (their signature dessert made from wheat flour dough with honey), and fresh water was provided, brought from one of the new wells.

Although Grace would have preferred a nice juicy steak or lobster, she ate the food and commented on how delicious it was.

When dinner was over, the people formed a large circle around the statue. King Ayu took Grace by the arm and led her to the center with him.

"What you are about to see, Miss Grace, is something that not many people are blessed to see."

Grace thought perhaps it was a special type of celebration dance or form of worship, but she never expected to see what would happen next.

As the people sang and danced, Grace thought she heard a baby cry. She didn't see any newborn children, so she dismissed it. A few minutes later, she heard the cry again, but this time much louder.

The cry was coming from up ahead. She saw two men holding the legs of a small struggling baby lamb. As the one man cut the lamb's neck and blood began draining into a golden chalice, Grace's knees buckled to the ground.

"*Stop*! What are you doing? Why did you kill the baby lamb?" she cried.

King Ayu answered, "This is an honor, Grace. You are witnessing something that many people never get to see."

Grace thought, *You got that right!* as the king continued to say, "You see, the killing and offering of one or more animals is part of our religious ritual. Back in the old days, God required animal sacrifices as a way for His people to temporarily atone for their sins and draw nearer to Him. Animal sacrifice was a deeply symbolic ritual. Blood, representing life, was to be drained from the animal, reminding worshippers of death. The sprinkling of blood around the Tabernacle represented life cleansing the death of sin, since blood was a symbol of life."

Grace could accept when an animal was killed to feed the starving people, but this was too much for her. Just then, one of the tribesmen brought the cup of blood to the king. As he began to drink it, a trickle of blood ran down his mouth. That was the last thing Grace remembered.

***

This was the second time in her life that Grace had fainted. The first was at the Academy Awards when she discovered Mattia had died and now seeing the king drink the blood of a lamb.

When Grace came to, she was lying on a cot that belonged to the mother of Aamina and Langa—the two small children she met earlier.

The woman's name was Aba, and she was a twenty-year-old widow. Aba's husband, Kanye, died shortly after his son Langa was born, leaving his teenage wife alone to raise their two young children.

One day, while Kanye was hunting food for his family, a rabid raccoon attacked and infected him with Baylisascaris (worms that are intestinal parasites).

During the struggle, Kanye ingested some of the animal's waste in his mouth. When he returned to the family hut, Kanye became nauseous and tired, and two weeks later, he expired from the deadly infection.

The hut Aba and her two small children lived in was nothing more than one room built of sticks and leaves. The roof was made of shingles, and the hut floor was mere compacted sand.

Togo has a dry climate and characteristics of a tropical savanna. Generally, there are two seasons of rain—the first one takes place between April and July and the second between October and November.

Luckily, Togo did not get hurricanes or cyclones, so in general, Togo remains warm and sunny year-round.

Outside of slender-snouted crocodiles that occasionally visited the villages, the African wild dog and the hyena were the most dangerous predators. One night, an African wild dog weighing eighty pounds snuck into the village and attacked and devoured a six-month-old baby. When Grace heard this, she was devastated.

After the day of the celebration, Grace began visiting Aba and her children every week. She would bring the mother whatever food she could, and they soon became good friends. One day, when Grace went to their hut, Langa was lying on the hard ground screaming while Aamina was crying hysterically. Nowhere in sight could Grace find their mother, Aba.

"Honey, where is your mama?" Grace asked the girl as she picked her baby brother up.

Both children were covered in feces, and it was hard to

see their faces from the filth that was encrusted on them.

A woman from a nearby hut ran over and told Grace, "Mama went home to our God in the sky to be with her husband."

"What? When?"

"Two days ago. She was attacked and killed by a hippo as she was washing her family's clothes in the river. It was terrible! A female hippo was protecting her baby in the water and attacked poor Aba and crushed her. Our men tried to save her, but were unable."

After gathering herself, Grace said, "Who has been taking care of her children for the past two days? They are screaming and filthy."

"Nobody. We hardly have enough food for our own."

Grace was appalled. She went back to the hut and took both of Abba's children with her as she hailed a taxi to King Ayu's home.

"Good morning, Grace. And who do we have here?" he asked, looking at the children.

"King Ayu, these are my friend Aba's children: Aamina and Langa. Their mother was killed two days ago by a hippo, and they have been alone since then."

The king had one of his servants take the children to bathe and feed them.

"What will happen to these children now?" Grace asked.

"Unfortunately, they will go to the local orphanage to live their lives out. Since Togo is the tenth poorest country in the world, 50 percent of the children are orphans."

When she left the king's home, Grace drove to the orphanage with the two children. The caretaker, Sister Mina, was there to greet them.

"*Karibu*," the pleasant woman said welcoming them.

Inside a dilapidated building were thirty or more small children huddled together. The tiny room reeked of urine and feces. Mother Mina was the only woman there. She appeared to be about fifty years old.

Inside there were about thirty children ranging from the ages of six months to ten years old.

Mother Mina said that children from all villages were sent to her. The neonatal mortality rate was tragic, as 50 percent die every year from famine, disease, pneumonia, and neglect.

"This is inhumane. Someone has to do something about this horrific situation."

And Grace Gambino did!

PART VI:

A DESTINY FULFILLED

"Return unto thy rest, O my soul; for the Lord hath dealt bountifully with thee" (Psalm 116:7).

CHAPTER 24

One day, while inspecting the completion of a water well, Grace heard a strange whimpering sound coming from behind debris left by the workers. At first, she thought it must be a kitten that perhaps wandered away from its mother—but the closer she got, the cries became louder and more human-like.

When Grace reached the area where the noise was coming from she was shocked at what she discovered. Lying in the dirt was a very small baby girl who couldn't have been much older than a few months old.

Frantic, Grace picked up the frightened, shivering infant and covered her with Grace's sweater. She looked around for the child's mother, but there was no one around.

She held the baby girl and went to the closest village, asking if anybody knew the infant or who it belonged to, and was shocked to find that this type of incident was not unusual. Fatima, an elder woman in the village, said that more and more of these heartbreaking events have been happening lately.

"Sometimes, when a single mother is dying or too sick to care for her child, she abandons it. Some of these women believe that God will intercept and save it, while others abandon the baby because they don't want the child to watch them die. Just last week, two brothers from our village found an infant who had been buried alive and dug up by dogs. Obviously, the baby didn't survive, for she had been devoured by the wild dogs," cried Fatima.

"This can't be real! This is simply inhumane! We have to stop this. Children are innocent living creatures that didn't ask to be brought into the world and discarded like trash. There are too many unwanted babies here. Something has to be done *now*!"

Grace took the abandoned baby girl with her and immediately went back to King Ayu's home. Surprised to see Grace for the second time that day, the king said, "Miss Grace, all I can do is put this baby girl in the orphanage where she most likely will remain her entire life. There are so many babies being born here in Togo, and when a parent cannot keep it due to an illness or simply cannot afford to feed and clothe it, the mother feels that they are better off 'in God's hands.'"

"In God's hands! King Ayu, forgive me for saying this, but this is *not* how our Lord wants these innocent babies treated."

"Unfortunately, we cannot keep and feed every baby

who is born here."

Astounded, Grace replied, "Why don't your people practice some kind of birth control?"

"Birth control! That's funny. The only birth control we have here is to sustain from the act. And that's not going to happen. In the village, girls begin engaging in sex as early as twelve years old. Sometimes, it is consensual, but most of the time, it is not. When men or boys get that desire, they grab whatever girl they can—whether or not the girls consent to it."

"What do you mean? Are the children raped? By whom?"

"Sadly it is usually by a relative. Either a father, uncle, or brother."

"This is so primitive! We are not living in the Dark Ages—this is the twenty-first century! You cannot allow this type of thing to happen, King."

"I cannot be in more than one place. My job is to rule my people, not watch if they are engaging in sex."

"You *must* do something. This cannot continue. And what will happen to this baby girl?" asked Grace.

"She will live in our orphanage for the rest of her life. Sadly, we only have one small orphanage that now houses around thirty children, and there is only one woman to care for them. There are an estimated three and a half million orphans in South Africa alone. They are orphaned when their father, mother, or both parents die. Some are orphaned when their parents die from Ebola, cholera, or AIDS. In the world, there are 140 million orphans. In Africa, 52 million make up more than 30 percent of the entire orphan population. The babies that survive might grow up turning to a family member for support, but they are usually unable to provide it."

The baby in Grace's arms was a beautiful girl. She appeared to be interracial, for her skin was a shade of caramel.

After leaving King Ayu, Grace drove back to the orphanage for the second time that day.

Mother Mina welcomed her, but it was obvious she was overworked and tired. The only thing the children wore was a ragged piece of clothing so old and soiled you couldn't tell what color it once was.

"What's going to happen to this baby?" Grace asked the woman.

"She will end up like the others here. Chances are she will never be adopted. The thirty years I have been working here there has never been one baby ever adopted," Mother Mina said. "And the ones that may be taken in by a relative are often sexually mistreated or sold."

"*Sold*? What do you mean?"

"Miss Grace, today, children are being sold as slaves for as little as thirty-seven dollars. This is the same price as a cow! Boys and girls can be sold many times over and in different ways for profit. The majority of child slaves work seven days a week with no or little pay, and twenty-two thousand children are killed at work every year—more than two children every hour!"

"Well, whatever I can do to end this barbaric situation, I will!"

***

After the day Grace found the abandoned baby, she devoted all of her time and effort to helping to end child slavery in Africa and humanizing the situation for the orphans.

Grace adopted the baby, who she now called Zuri—which means "good and beautiful." Grace didn't want the girl to grow up in a hotel, so she met with several local building contractors to construct a large, new orphanage and build her a small house in Togo where she and Zuri would live. Eighteen months later, the orphanage was completed. It would be called The Saving Grace Orphanage.

Inside the five-room house were bunk beds and mattresses with clean bed linens, a long table with chairs for the children to eat on and washing machines to clean their clothes.

It was clean and spacious, and Grace hired four more women from the village to help Mother Mina care for the children.

Zuri was now two years old and had brought nothing but

joy and love to Grace. The mother and child had developed a very strong bond as Grace saw a lot of herself in Zuri, for the girl was independent and strong-willed—just like her adoptive mother.

Ever since Grace built the water wells and orphanage, Togo was a much better, safer, and happier place to live. Several years after the new orphanage was built, Grace opened a small school in the village where she shared the Gospel with the staff and children.

The Grace of God Baptist Church opened as the light of the gospel continued to grow. A number of villagers (including a well-known witch doctor) attended weekly, and they all gave their lives to Jesus.

Grace was no longer known as the new Sophia Loren, the world's most famous model, or the girl with the butterfly tattoo. She was now known as Mother Grace.

CHAPTER 25
TOGO, AFRICA
2004

Reminiscing the chapters of my life and the many blessings God has bestowed on me, I realize now that all the fame and wealth I once took pride in has become meaningless.

Pride is a heart-attitude sin that overflows into one's imagination and activities. It stems from self-righteousness and consumes the person so that their thoughts are far from God.

Material things that are stolen or lost can be found or bought again, but there is only one thing that can never be found when it's lost—and that is life. And I can assure you that the only one who will never leave your side or abandon you is our Holy Heavenly Father.

As I sit here watching God's magnificent creatures roam the African grasslands, I thank my heavenly Father for the blessed life He has bestowed on me. Granted, it hasn't been all smooth sailing, for I've certainly had my share of heartaches, disappointments, and grief, as almost everyone has.

I never knew my birth parents, so I guess you could say I'm an orphan, but when I was five months old, a wonderful couple adopted me and gave me the best life they possibly could.

I no longer look like the stunning movie star I once was or the sexy model that graced the cover of Sports Illustrated. I have not worn designer clothes in decades as my only wardrobe consists of two plain dresses one of the villagers made for me.

No longer are Jimmy Choo or Christian Louboutin shoes on my feet; instead, my only pair of shoes is a pair of leather sandals my friend Zala, the village blacksmith, made especially for me. They are very special, for across the top are two leather straps to resemble my favorite thing—a butterfly.

The only people outside of Togo I have contact with today are my best friends, Tianna, Antone, and little Gabby, who is not so little anymore. She is now a beautiful twenty-two-year-old woman who runs Anna's Butterfly Sanctuary in my hometown of Palermo.

Anna's Butterfly Sanctuary has become world-renowned, as people from all over the planet visit it yearly to learn about the wonderful little creature my Lord etched *into my skin before I was born.*

In fact, Anna's Butterfly Sanctuary is one of the world's most popular travel destinations—rating right up there with Disneyland, the Eiffel Tower, and the Vatican!

Can you believe that an orphaned baby grew up to help millions of people discover and enjoy the wonderful creature called a butterfly? And besides bringing fresh water wells to many villages throughout Africa, hundreds of orphaned babies will have the opportunity to live a normal life with people who love them and make a positive impact in the world.

They learn about the Lord and give their lives to Jesus, and some have even become ministers, nuns, teachers, and missionaries.

My daughter, Zuri, is an intelligent, beautiful woman—inside and out—who helps to carry on my legacy. I am very proud of her.

I know she could have been a famous model herself for her exotic looks have captured the attention of many modeling agencies and producers.

After her photo appeared on the cover of the New York Times when they did a story on the orphanage, the phones rang off the wall from modeling agencies and Hollywood directors. I told Zuri the decision was hers to make, but the Lord had His hand on her to do His work instead.

I haven't been feeling well lately and am having trouble focusing. The village doctor is on his way here, so God willing, I will get some good news, but I know that no matter what he tells me, God is in control and has His hand on me.

I do not fear death, for I have done everything God wanted me to. I am actually looking forward to going back home so that I can see my adoptive parents, the parents I never knew, my grandparents, my beloved Mattia, and of course, Max, my precious little dog.

But until that day, I will continue doing God's work and pray that when the day comes for me to return home, my Lord will be waiting by the gates, saying, "Well done, good and faithful servant. You have been faithful over a little; I will set you over much. Enter into the joy of your master" (Matthew 25:21, ESV).

CHAPTER 26

Coincidentally? No! Grace Gambino Antonelli did *not* believe in coincidences.

It was on July 4, 2004, when Grace took ill. It was on her fiftieth birthday when she was diagnosed with malaria after being bitten by a mosquito.

When she began getting severe headaches and chills, Grace thought it was merely the flu she had picked up from one of the children in the orphanage, but when the symptoms got worse, Grace's daughter, Zuri, contacted the village physician.

The witch doctor began treating Grace with natural remedies, such as medicinal plants, which seemed to be working at first, but when Grace took a turn for the worse, Zuri sent for Dr. Okoro, a malaria specialist from Ghana.

When the doctor observed Grace's red blood cells under the microscope, he saw the malaria parasite that looked like a blue signet ring. The presence of the parasites in the blood caused the symptoms of fever, chills, body aches, and headache—all of which Grace exhibited. The parasite affected Grace's liver as it quickly grew and multiplied.

Malaria was the leading cause of hospitalization and the leading cause of death in Africa. It was an epidemic with a transmission that lasted almost a year throughout the national territory.

In 2000, an estimated four hundred thousand people died from malaria—mostly young children in sub-Saharan Africa, and when Grace began burying friends who had caught malaria, she donated a substantial amount of money to find a cure.

The irony is that Grace was especially careful to use all precautions against the disease, such as protective clothing for the children, getting them vaccinated, and using bed nets to keep the mosquitos away from the possibility of one entering the orphanage and infecting a child.

That was just like Grace—always looking out for others before herself.

When Dr. Okoro diagnosed Grace with *P. Falciparum*—the species that causes the most complications and has the highest mortality rate, he recommended Grace be transported to Saint Mary's Hospital in Johannesburg.

"If you don't get immediate treatment, Mother Grace, you will not live longer than a month."

"Zulu—please listen to the doctor," Zuri begged her mother.

"Honey, I am leaving my life in God's hands as I've always done. If it is my turn to go home, I'm ready. I have accomplished everything the Lord asked me to. I have had a wonderful life, and if it is time to go to my heavenly home, so be it."

For the next few weeks, Zuri watched her mother slowly fade away. Once a healthy-looking woman, Grace was now down to ninety pounds. Her gaunt appearance made it hard to believe she was once called "the most beautiful woman in the world."

Her organs began to fail, causing her liver and kidneys to rupture, and anemia set in. The accumulation of fluid in her lungs made it difficult for Grace to breathe.

One day, while Grace was sitting outside the orphanage watching the animals roam the land, the sky suddenly turned black. It had not rained for weeks and was not forecast for that day. Clouds appeared to open while a double rainbow appeared in the sky. The Togolese became alarmed—not sure of what was happening.

As the sky turned darker, it began to lightly rain—but only onto Grace. A beam of radiant light shone down from heaven, and at that moment, a beautiful emerald swallowtail butterfly flew from the sky onto Grace's shoulder.

Its wings were covered with a large set of green scales with the background color varying from dark green to black and a broad set of bright emerald green metallic bands that formed in an almost V shape. The butterfly was the exact color of Grace's eyes.

In awe of its beauty and realizing that once again this was "a whisper from God," Grace muttered, *"I'm ready, my Lord. Take me home."* As the fluttering butterfly clapped his wings, Grace Gambino smiled and breathed her final breath.

EPILOGUE

The day that Grace Gambino Antonelli, also known as the girl with the butterfly tattoo, died, the Togolese people mourned. After observing the sky turn dark, the rain falling only onto Grace, and a butterfly that appeared from nowhere landing on her shoulder, they thought it was indeed a miracle from God. The Togolese all knelt down and gave praise to the heavenly Father, calling it a true phenomenon.

When Zuri called Tianna and Antone, they immediately booked a flight and flew to Africa with their daughter, Gabrielle. According to the African belief system, life does not end with death but continues to another realm. They believed in the existence after death, in the power and role of the deceased ancestor, and in the ones left behind going through a grieving process.

Death is often looked at from both religious and cultural perspectives in Africa. Based on this system of belief, those who are dead are alive in a different world. After death, an individual lives in a spirit world, receiving a new body with the capacity to move about as an ancestor. With the belief that the goal of life is to become an ancestor after death, a person is given a proper burial after death, as a failure to do this may result in the individual becoming a ghost.

Since Grace was a devout Christian, she knew that life is

not our own—it is fragile and limited. The Bible recognizes death as the end of life and the severer of relationships.

Grace was brought up to believe that what happens after death is dependent on the choices you make in your life. That is why Grace had always lived a godly life.

The day after Zuri called Tianna, they flew to Africa and were met at the airport by the young woman. Although the two women had talked on the phone many times, this was the first time they had met in person.

When they arrived at the village, the villagers were singing and dancing for they were having a celebration of life in honor of Mother Grace. The celebration of life lasted one week.

Although Tianna wanted to fly Grace's body back to Palermo to bury her alongside her grandparents, Zuri told Ti that Grace's last wish was to remain in Africa.

A lot of planning went into Grace Gambino Antonelli's funeral. There would be gospel hymns, fervent prayers, and spirited processions to honor their beloved Mother Grace's ascension to heaven to live forever under the rule of Jesus Christ.

An essential component of an African funeral is having the deceased's actual body available to be carried triumphantly to the cemetery for burial. Although it was not something a normal African funeral provides—because this was Mother Grace's—King Aye commissioned the most elegant casket designed for her.

Behind the orphanage, a mausoleum was erected. The king commissioned the construction of Grace's final resting place to resemble that of the Mausoleum of Mohammed V. The building's architecture and interior design were particularly striking, featuring a granite floor, a carved ceiling, and a skylight to let heaven's light shine down in. On the side of the mausoleum stood a life-size bronze statue of Grace with the writing, "The Girl With The Butterfly Tattoo."

The day Grace was laid to rest was sunny and hot. Everyone from the village was there to pay their respect. Gabrielle held hands with Zuri as both women cried uncontrollably.

Tianna told Gabby, "Honey, Aunt Grace would not want you to be sad. She would want you to celebrate her life—and what a life she had. There was and never will be another Grace Gambino. She was the most beautiful woman—inside and out—our Lord ever created. And Zuri, your mother's entire life, all she wanted was someone to love her for the person she was inside—not just because she was beautiful outside. When she called and told me about you, I had never heard her so happy. She was so proud of the woman you had grown up to be and loved you more than anything in the world. She was so blessed to have you call her mother. Grace loved God, life, and everyone she ever met. She didn't have a bad bone in her body and was and always will be my best friend."

Eight of the village men carried the casket en route to

Grace's final resting place as the women, dressed in bright colors, danced and sang.

When the procession reached the mausoleum, an eerie feeling overcame the villagers as the sky once again turned black.

It began to rain lightly as a beautiful double rainbow appeared in the sky.

From the heavens, hundreds of butterflies appeared and flew down, landing on top of the casket.

Everyone, including King Aye, was taken aback at what they had just witnessed. Some women got on their knees and prayed while others cried.

Tianna smiled as she touched the casket. "It's okay, Gracie, to go home now. You have been God's greatest ambassador and have changed the world and everyone you met for the better. Fly high, my beautiful butterfly—you are now free."

At that moment, every butterfly flew off the casket into the sky until they could no longer be seen as a brilliant light shone down from above.

Grace Gambino was finally home.

Other Christian books written by Victoria M. Howard

The Stairway to Heaven

Vivian and Max—Little Ambassadors for Christ

Whispers From God

The Evolution of V

Snow Right and the Seven Angels

ABOUT THE AUTHOR

Victoria Howard has been a model, racehorse trainer, professional dancer, and beauty queen winner who once represented her state in the Mrs. USA Pageant.

She has penned twenty-five books and appeared on Fox & Friends, Good Morning Sacramento, Good Day L.A., and Good Day Kentucky.

After surviving a double pulmonary embolism, Victoria knew there was something left she needed to do with her life, so she returned to school and received a Doctorate in Christian Bereavement Counseling and also became an ordained minister.